Welcome to the Cooper Academy of Detection and Espionage

"Look here, Pickle. There's a handle. The side of the platform is a door! Oh my! I think we've done it! I think we've found the entrance!"

Grabbing hold of the handle, and with a considerable shove of her shoulder, Wilma pushed open the secret door and the plucky pair found themselves standing in a doorway that led into a corridor. They were inside the Academy at last.

"Help," sounded a voice, somewhere in the distance. "Hello! Help!"

An unknown voice calling for help? Someone in trouble? But who? And why? You'll just have to read on. Cancel all your plans. This is going to get chilly.

Other Books You May Enjoy

Wilma Tenderfoot

The Case of the Putrid Poison

by Emma Kennedy

PUFFIN BOOKS
An Imprint of Penguin Group (USA) Inc.

PUFFIN BOOKS

Published by the Penguin Group

Penguin Young Readers Group, 345 Hudson Street, New York, New York 10014, U.S.A.

Penguin Group (Canada), 90 Eglinton Avenue East, Suite 700, Toronto, Ontario, Canada M4P 2Y3

(a division of Pearson Penguin Canada Inc.)

Penguin Books Ltd, 80 Strand, London WC2R 0RL, England

Penguin Ireland, 25 St Stephen's Green, Dublin 2, Ireland (a division of Penguin Books Ltd)

Penguin Group (Australia), 250 Camberwell Road, Camberwell, Victoria 3124, Australia

(a division of Pearson Australia Group Pty Ltd)

Penguin Books India Pvt Ltd, 11 Community Centre, Panchsheel Park, New Delhi – 110 017, India

Penguin Group (NZ), 67 Apollo Drive, Rosedale, Auckland 0632, New Zealand

(a division of Pearson New Zealand Ltd.)

Penguin Books (South Africa) (Pty) Ltd, 24 Sturdee Avenue, Rosebank,

Johannesburg 2196, South Africa

Penguin Books Ltd, Registered Offices: 80 Strand, London WC2R 0RL, England

Published in the United Kingdom by Macmillan Children's Books UK, 2010
First published in the United States of America by Dial Books for Young Readers, 2011
Published by Puffin Books, a member of Penguin Young Readers Group, 2012

1 3 5 7 9 10 8 6 4 2

Copyright © Emma Kennedy, 2010
All rights reserved

THE LIBRARY OF CONGRESS HAS CATALOGED THE DIAL EDITION AS FOLLOWS:
Kennedy, Emma.
The case of the putrid poison / by Emma Kennedy.
p. cm. — (Wilma Tenderfoot ; 2)
Summary: As apprentice detective to Theodore Goodman, Wilma, a ten-year-old orphan of
Cooper Island's Lowside Institute for Woeful Children, helps investigate who is poisoning actors
at the Valiant Vaudeville Theatre, but when Theodore disappears, she must take action on her own.
ISBN 978-0-8037-3541-5 (hc)
[1. Actors and actresses—Fiction. 2. Theaters—Fiction. 3. Poisons—Fiction. 4. Missing persons—
Fiction. 5. Orphans—Fiction. 6. England—Fiction. 7. Mystery and detective stories.] I. Title.
PZ7.K3776Cap 2011
[Fic]—dc22   2011001165

Puffin Books ISBN 978-0-14-242141-3

Text set in Perpetua

Printed in the United States of America

PEARSON

For Itsy and Sydney

Thank you

As ever, I'd like to wave overenthusiastically in the direction of my brilliant agent, Camilla Hornby, without whom I would be a bag of dust. Not only that, but thanks of a massive nature must be hurled down a steep hillside toward my amazing editor, Ruth Alltimes, who makes everything better, and Samantha Swinnerton, who has been simply fabulous.

The Case of the Putrid Poison

"Of course I realize now," said Wilma, consulting her Clue Ring, "that we have made a terrible error, Pickle. In the Case of the Decoy Duck, Mr. Goodman *also* set out to rescue a cat that seemed to be trapped up a tree, but, unlike us, he soon deducted that cats can jump from trees quite happily. Which we cannot. Well, that's that. We're stuck."

Pickle, who was hanging on to a branch by his teeth for dear life, was in no doubt about it. This was his most embarrassing moment to date. Here he was, swinging precariously from a tree and being stared at by the cat that had, only moments before, seemed in the gravest peril but was now happily sitting in the garden of Clarissa Cottage with not a care in the world. Like most dogs, Pickle had a natural suspicion of cats, so being stared at by one while in slightly shaming circumstances was more than any dog could bear. The cat shot Pickle a look of complete disdain and sauntered off with an arrogant twitch of its tail. Oh! This was AWFUL!

Wilma, whose hair was peppered with broken twigs, looked down at her embarrassed beagle. "How long do you think you can hang on, Pickle?" she asked, trying to edge her way toward him along a particularly creaky bough. "I hope Mr. Goodman doesn't see us. Now that I'm his apprentice I should be trying to detect things properly. But, remembering Mr. Goodman's top tips for detectives, I don't think I contemplated or deducted. It's a schoolgirl error, Pickle. And now I'm going to catch it."

Wilma Tenderfoot was a small but determined girl. Brought up as an orphan at the revolting

Lowside Institute for Woeful Children, she had spent all of her life longing to get away and be like her hero Theodore P. Goodman, Cooper Island's most famous and serious detective. He had a very impressive mustache and a woeful weakness for corn crumble biscuits and peppermint tea. But don't let that bother you now. This is the background bit. Pickle was Wilma's beagle. He had one tatty ear and a reckless love of tidbits. They had met in a dusty basement in unfortunate circumstances and, as anyone knows, encounters in dark places with dirty dogs and raggedy children always lead to immediate friendships. Those are the rules.

Due to a series of alarming events involving a stolen stone and a lot of frozen hearts, Wilma, who had been sent away by the Institute's ghastly matron, Madam Skratch, to work for an equally ghastly mistress called Mrs. Waldock, had found herself unexpectedly taken on as Mr. Goodman's apprentice. It was a dream come true and she was single-minded in her resolve to be the best apprentice on Cooper. For those of you wondering where Cooper is, all that can be revealed is that it's somewhere between England and France and that if you look hard enough you'll find it. Having said that, Cooper is yet to be discovered by the outside world. There was once a close encounter with a ship captained by Horatio Nelson (the famous columnist), but it was a foggy day, so let's cut the man some slack. He only had one eye. He can't be expected to see everything.

The other thing you need to know is that at the precise moment that Wilma became Theodore's apprentice, there was what we in the trade call a "massive revelation." This is something that induces sharp intakes of breath and causes ladies of a certain disposition to say "Ooooooh!" and indulge in a lot of sudden nudging. In Wilma's case, the massive revelation was that somewhere, perhaps on Cooper itself, she had a relative who was still alive. Imagine that! But let's not get distracted. For now, Wilma and Pickle are stuck up a tree and neither of them knows what to do about it.

This was a bad business. Wilma had only been

with Mr. Goodman for a week and hadn't had much to do in the way of detecting. So the small ginger cat stuck in the old pear tree at the bottom of Clarissa Cottage garden seemed the perfect opportunity to get her new job up and running, but instead here she was in another small but sticky mess.

"Wilma!" came the voice of Mrs. Speckle, Theodore's not-to-be-messed-with housekeeper. "Where are you? A letter's arrived. Got your name on it!"

"A letter?" mumbled Wilma, trying to get her leg around a particularly fulsome patch of blossom. "Who would have sent me a letter? Oh dear, Pickle. Matters are taking an urgent turn and here we are stuck in sticks."

Pickle said nothing. But then he couldn't. His mouth was currently occupied and very much unavailable.

As Mrs. Speckle's calls boomed from the kitchen, Wilma realized that being caught in the upper branches of an increasingly unstable pear tree with one small dog hanging by his teeth was not the sort of First Week Best Start that any apprentice should hope for. It wouldn't do at all for her to call for help or set in motion a chain of events that some might later be able to refer to as a minor emergency. No. Wilma would have to solve this scrape herself. From extensive and frequent readings of her Clue Ring, the collection of newspaper and magazine articles about Theodore's exploits that she carried everywhere on a metal hoop on her pinafore, Wilma knew that the answer to drawing any slight crisis to a close was invariably to be found within reaching distance.

Pushing an unwieldy and dangerously bouncy branch out of her face, Wilma squinted downward. "Ooooh," she said, wobbling. "I wish I hadn't done that. We're actually quite high up, Pickle. Let's try not to think about that."

Keeping one arm firmly around the pear tree's trunk, which was now emitting worrying and alarming groans, Wilma used the other to clear a peephole through some leaves. Just above her, at the top of the tree, she could see the tail end of a piece of rope. "That must be the climbing rope for bringing down the pears," she said, jumping a little to reach it. The tree gave out another shuddering moan. "There's something very wrong with this tree," she exclaimed. "If I was a proper detective, which I'm not yet, but I will be one day, then I would deduce that this is an old tree that may or may not be in grave danger of coming down. Not to worry you or anything."

Dogs don't have eyebrows, which is a terrible shame, but, if they did, then Pickle's would have been as far up his forehead as they were physically capable of being.

As Wilma pulled the rope toward her, she gave it a tug to check it was tethered good and tight. Satisfied that the rope was secure, she looped it once around her left wrist and then, using it to steady herself, made her way toward Pickle. "Get ready, Pickle," she said. "I'm going to use this rope to jump down and I'm going to grab you as I go. We'll be out of this tree in no time."

The branch Wilma was tiptoeing along began to tremble and judder. Wilma gulped. She'd clearly have to ignore that. It is a general truth that when in a tree that appears to be falling down, it's often best to get on with things and try not to think about the worst that could happen.

Pickle was now in reach, so Wilma, clinging to the rope, heaved herself off the shuddering branch. Swinging by her wrist, she scooped Pickle up in her spare arm, closed her eyes, and hoped for the best. But what Wilma had failed to do was tell Pickle to let go, so as they careened down toward the ground, the upper part of the tree, pulled by the branch that Pickle was still biting, came with them.

There was a loud, splintering crack and as the old pear tree split at its base, it cleaved sideways and sent Wilma and Pickle splattering to the lawn.

"Well," panted Wilma, shoving a leafy mass out of her face. "Technically, we're still in the tree. But at least we're on the ground. You can let go now," she added, noting that a traumatized Pickle was still clenched to his branch.

"Wilma!" shouted Mrs. Speckle again, peering from the kitchen window. "Where are you?"

"Coming, Mrs. Speckle!" yelled Wilma, crawling out from under the mass of broken branches. "Don't say a word about the pear tree," she added, giving Pickle a conspiratorial nod. "If anyone's suspicious, we'll just blame the wind."

The letter that had arrived was addressed to:

Wilma Tenderfoot

c/o Theodore P. Goodman,
Cooper Island's Most Serious and Famous Detective

On its top right-hand corner there was a crest of a magnifying glass crossed with a false mustache. The letter had been picked off the doormat by Mrs. Speckle, dressed head to toe in her trademark woolen outfit, and was waiting to be delivered to the young apprentice on a knitted tray. Everything Mrs. Speckle wore was made from wool, from the watch on her wrist to the spectacles on her face. If it wasn't warm, it wasn't wanted. As Wilma bounced into the kitchen, still spitting out bits of leaf and covered in all manner of tree-based detritus, her employer, Theodore P. Goodman, was standing waiting for his peppermint tea, an afternoon drink, you will remember, to which he was overwhelmingly partial.

"Goodness," he said, casting his young apprentice a long glance. Her blond, scruffy hair was a tangle of leaves, her pinafore was covered in grassy smudges, her socks were scrunched down to her ankles, and her knees were smothered in mud. "You look as if you've been dragged through a bush backward."

"It was a tree, actually," said Wilma suddenly, without thinking. Pickle rolled his eyes. So much for keeping quiet.

"A tree?" asked Mrs. Speckle suspiciously, picking up the tray and shoving it under Wilma's nose.

"Never mind," said Wilma, remembering she wasn't supposed to say anything. "Is that letter for me?" she asked quickly, blowing a caterpillar out from her hair.

"Well, it's addressed to you," interjected Theodore, reaching for the pipe in his pocket. "Looks quite official, I'd say. You'd better open it."

Wilma had never received a proper letter before. She stared at the envelope as it lay on the tray and experienced what some people might call a hullabaloo.

"I'm very nervous," she said eventually, twisting the bottom of her pinafore. "But, actually, I'm quite excited at the same time. Like the inside of a sparkly drink. Or a bag of bees. Or a load of bubbles. Or . . ."

"Yes, I get the drift, Wilma," answered Theodore P. Goodman, packing his pipe with some rosemary tobacco. "That'll do. I suggest you calm yourself. Remember, apprentice detectives don't get to be proper detectives unless they are contemplative and occasionally silent."

"I can try and be contemplative," said Wilma, bouncing up and down. "But I don't know if I can do the silent bit quite yet. I'm too full of fizz."

"Oh, just open it," grumbled Mrs. Speckle, still holding out the tray. "My arm's getting tired."

Wilma gulped and picked the embossed envelope up off the tray. Breaking the seal on the back, she opened it carefully and read it out loud.

Dear Wilma Tenderfoot,

You are cordially invited to have a crack at the Entrance Exam for the Cooper Academy of Detection and Espionage. The exam will take place in three days' time. Please be at the Academy at 8:30 a.m. sharpish. You will need:

1. some comfy shoes
2. some loose-fitting clothes, breathable and kicky
3. a couple of corn crumbles and
4. a small white paper bag that smells of pear candies.

I look forward to meeting you (maybe) and good luck.

Yours sincerely,

Kite Lambard
(Headmistress)

P.S. Clue number one: It's obvious, when you think about it.

Wilma was beside herself. "The Academy of Detection and Espionage?" she asked, wide-eyed. "I didn't even know there was such a thing! Is it brilliant? Do they have the biggest Clue Board in the universe? Who lives there? What's an espionage? Is it a sort of omelet?"

Theodore looked down his pipe at his young apprentice. "No, Wilma," he answered with as much patience as he could muster, "it is not an omelet. The Academy of Detection and Espionage is an important step for anyone wanting to be a detective. In fact, you can only be a proper detective if you are accepted. I went there, as did my mentor before me. Obviously you will learn a lot of practical skills from me during your apprenticeship, but it's also very important to learn the *theory* of detecting, which is what you will learn at the Academy. If you get in."

Wilma nodded. At this point she should have asked something sensible and detective-like, but she was far too excited. So when she asked, "If I get in to the Academy, will there be amazing things like horses that can sing?" Theodore, who despite fast becoming used to dealing with Wilma's incessant questions, realized that answering anything further would be more trouble than it was worth. Sometimes, great and serious detectives just need a modicum of quiet and so, with his small apprentice jumping at his feet, Theodore sighed, retired to his study, and very gently locked the door.

"Now you've done it," said Mrs. Speckle, shoving up her double-knitted cardigan sleeves. "Too many questions, young lady! Why don't you stop bothering poor Mr. Goodman and get on with your chores? There's plenty to be done! Less guessing and more doing! That's what I say!"

"Yes, Mrs. Speckle," answered Wilma, pulling a long twig out from behind her ear.

"What the blue blazes!" screamed Mrs. Speckle suddenly as she paused at the back door. "The old pear tree's down! Hang on a minute," she added, twisting on her knitted Wellington boots, "this wasn't your doing, was it, Tenderfoot?"

But for once Wilma had nothing to say. Nothing to say at all.

Sometimes, it's difficult for small and determined girls to stop their minds whirring, but Wilma knew she would have to contain her excitement. So far, during her short apprenticeship, all Wilma had been allowed to do was write out the labels for a few Clue Bags, which, despite being essential to the everyday requirements of a detective, were still just plain paper bags with no clues in them yet. In short, it was a chore that was neither dangerous nor daring. Perhaps, Wilma thought, as she sat with a heap of small bags in front of her, when she was enrolled in the

Academy she might progress to mightier tasks, like chalking outlines for dead bodies or even deducting in an official capacity. But that was all a long way off yet.

Before becoming Theodore's apprentice, Wilma had followed his every exploit by collecting newspaper and magazine clippings that she had found in Madam Skratch's wastepaper basket at the Institute. Through them she had learned about the detective's top tips, ten essential things that a budding detective should always do if he wants to solve any crime. There was eavesdropping, being circuitous, and Wilma's personal favorite—the use of disguises for cunning moments. Wilma had tried to emulate all of them as she chased after Theodore, trying to become his apprentice. She had done well, but now that she was a proper apprentice, her mentor had impressed upon her that scampering around in an unofficial role had to stop. It was time for her to behave seriously at all times (top tip number nine), to watch and learn and wait for instructions.

Having had a substantial breakfast (top tip

number ten—never go detecting on an empty stomach), Wilma was ready for her big day. If she wanted to be a proper detective, it was all very well knowing about the top tips, but unless she got in to the Academy, all her dreams would be dashed. So later that morning she stood before the immense building, with the biscuits in her pocket and a paper bag that smelled of pear candies in hand, ready to give it her best shot.

Standing with her, as always, was her faithful beagle Pickle, who was so nervous on Wilma's behalf he'd been making involuntary smells for half an hour. Her mentor, Theodore P. Goodman, had also accompanied her. He had put her name forward for the Academy and, as such, his presence was the right and proper thing to have. "Eight twenty-seven," he said, looking at his pocket watch. "I should leave you to it. Do your best. And if you get stuck, clear your mind and think logically."

"Yes, Mr. Goodman," answered Wilma, conjuring up her most serious face.

"There is always a simple answer to everything, Wilma," said Theodore, twiddling the end of his mighty mustache. "Don't forget that. Well, good-bye. And good luck." The great detective took Wilma's hand, shook it, and walked away.

Wilma took the letter from her pinafore pocket. "Eight thirty a.m. sharpish," she whispered. "I expect that's about now, Pickle. I suppose we'd better go in. I hope they've got pencils. I haven't brought one with me."

Pickle shook his head and made another smell. Generally speaking, small dogs don't do well under strict examination conditions, which is why they never try to learn to drive. Or become garden designers.

Wilma stared up at the Academy. The same crest that had been on the letter she was sent hung from two copper hooks above her. It was a curious box-shaped building, jet black with no windows and, even more puzzling, no front door. "Well, this is odd," said Wilma, looking at the blank wall in front of her. "How are we supposed to take the entrance exam if we can't get in? What did the letter say? 'It's obvious, when you think about it.' Well, I'm thinking as hard as I can, Pickle, and it's not obvious at all. How can I take the entrance exam if I can't find the entrance?"

Pickle gave a gentle whirrup and turned around on the spot. Wilma frowned and put her hands on her hips. "Just because I don't know what I'm doing," Wilma said, holding a finger aloft, "is no reason to give in! Pickle! I have made my mind up. It is obvious. The entrance exam is finding the entrance. Start sniffing!"

As the tatty-eared beagle put his nose to the ground, Wilma stood very still. "When Mr. Goodman is contemplating and deducting," she pronounced, "the first thing he does is remain in a quiet repose and look around him. He's always telling me that. I think this is reposing. So all I have to do now is look. Don't make a sound, Pickle. It's very important that we're practically silent."

Pickle, unsure how to snuffle the ground without making a noise, froze and hovered his nostrils over a discarded red brick in the hope that any incriminating smell might simply waft itself up. There was something, but without a deep, loud sniff he couldn't quite be sure. Wilma, eyes darting to the left and right, scanned the exterior of the Academy for clues.

The black expanse of the building's front wall rose above her. Intricate carvings adorned the exterior, and a few ebony gargoyles of Cooper's greatest detectives through history stared down from every corner. Frowning, Wilma could see nothing to help her. She gave a frustrated groan. "It's no good," she said, shaking her head. "I can't work it out. And you're being no help, Pickle. Stop fussing over that red brick! Wait! What's a red brick doing by a black building? Pickle! You're a genius!"

Wilma bent down to pick it up. The brick was heavy in her hand. "Well I never," she laughed, rubbing the dust away. "Look at that! Carved into the top! Oh, Pickle! This is thrilling!"

ALL BUILDINGS DEPEND ON THEIR FOUNDATIONS

"Foundations? Those are the things underground. The bits you can't see. Perhaps the entrance is somewhere beneath us? Like a tunnel?"

Wilma approached the front wall and began to look along the bottom of it for an underground opening. "Nothing," she murmured. "Wait! There's a sign down here. At the base of the building! What does it say, Pickle?"

Pickle stared at the tiny bronze plaque in front of him, but as much as he would have loved to help, there was nothing he could do. He'd forgotten his reading glasses. So that was that.

Wilma got down on to her hands and knees and peered at the wall.

ALL DELIVERIES PLEASE GO
TO REAR OF BUILDING

"Oh! Well, perhaps there isn't a tunnel. Perhaps there's an entrance there. Come on, Pickle, let's check."

Following a large stone finger that pointed toward "Rear of Building," the pair scampered

to the left and found themselves running alongside the building down a narrow alley. The alley
twisted around to the rear, and Wilma scanned
the back wall of the Academy for a door. But
there was no entrance to be seen. It was just
another blank wall.

"Nothing here!" Wilma yelled, throwing her
arms up in the air. "Oh, wait—there's a small
plaque."

REAR OF BUILDING
NO DELIVERIES, THANK YOU

"Oh, what's the point! This is crazy!"

Pickle, who had always held an odd affection
for alleys and backs of buildings, lifted his nose
and had a good sniff. In his experience, in places
like this there was usually an overflowing garbage
can to be found or a heap of tasty scraps. Wilma
leaned against the Academy wall with her arms
crossed. Heaving a sigh, she scuffed at the floor
with the end of her sandal. The beagle, convinced
he could smell an old chicken bone, wandered

off to the far end of the alley. With his nose to the ground, Pickle's sharp sense of smell led him, not to a delicious chewy bone, but to a rather revolting soggy sock. All the same, he *was* a bit peckish . . .

"There must be another clue here somewhere," said Wilma, following Pickle to the end of the alleyway. "Oh no, Pickle! How many times do I have to tell you!" she cried, reaching down. "Don't chew other people's lost socks!" Grabbing hold of the stinking sock, Wilma pulled it from Pickle's lips and flung it with some disgust toward the wall to her right. But as the revolting item hit the side of the Academy the wall's surface bent in on itself and, to Wilma's surprise, the sock bounced straight back and hit her in the mouth.

If you have ever had a stinking, wet sock that's been on who knows whose foot hit you full in the face, then you will know that as the dripping, smelly toe end slimed its way over Wilma's tongue, our young heroine experienced a disgust so complete that all she could do for the next five minutes was spin on the spot with her tongue out while trying to rub at it frantically with the end of her pinafore. Pickle just sat and stared at her. Stinking socks were lovely. She didn't know what she was missing.

Panting and satisfied that the last dregs of sock juice were expelled from her mouth, Wilma looked back at the wall where the sock had struck. "That sock shouldn't have bounced back," she said, peering a little closer.

She pressed her fingertips against the wall's surface, and suddenly realized that it was made from nothing more than a tightly drawn piece of material that had been painted to match its surroundings.

"It's just cloth!" Wilma exclaimed, eyes shining with excitement. "It's a secret covering! We must have to break through it! But how?" she added, tapping her foot. "Ah-ha!" she declared with a snap of her fingers. "I've got a safety pin in my pocket! I can use that!"

Taking the pin from her pinafore pocket, Wilma opened it out and stabbed at the camouflaged surface. The wall made a popping noise as the tension left it. Dragging the pin downward, Wilma made a hole large enough to fit both her hands. Reaching in, she grabbed either side of the cloth, tore with all her might, and poked her head in through the gap. "Oh my goodness," she panted. "It's not a door. It's a hidden recess. And there's a statue in here!"

The statue was standing on a platform that was a little taller than Wilma. It was of a man, tall and noble-looking. In one hand he was holding a magnifying glass aloft and in the other a small plate that seemed to be covered in what Wilma could only assume were carved stone corn crumbles. "Biscuits AND a magnifying glass?" she thought out loud. "He must be a detective. Yes, look! There's another plaque here."

ANTHONY AMBER, FOUNDER OF THE ACADEMY OF DETECTION AND ESPIONAGE

"That's it! He's the founder! All buildings depend on their foundations. A foundation can be a beginning! It's just like Mr. Goodman says. He's always using words that mean lots of things at once. It's a cunning detective thing. Wait a minute . . . Look here, Pickle. There's a handle. The side of the platform is a door! Oh my! I think we've done it! I think we've found the entrance!"

Grabbing hold of the handle, and with a considerable shove of her shoulder, Wilma pushed open the secret door and the plucky pair found themselves standing in a doorway that led into a corridor. They were inside the Academy at last.

"Help," sounded a voice, somewhere in the distance. "Hello! Help!"

An unknown voice calling for help? Someone in trouble? But who? And why? You'll just have to read on. Cancel all your plans. This is going to get chilly.

Wilma and Pickle had stepped straight into the corridor. The floor was covered with tiles painted with question marks, and a large mirror in the shape of a magnifying glass hung on the wall opposite the doorway. Portraits of great detectives lined the hallway. "Look, Pickle!" whispered Wilma, pointing upward. "It's Mr. Goodman! And look there! It's the detective's top tips! Carved into that stone tablet! Number five: 'When escaping, be circuitous.' That's my second-favorite."

Pickle snorted. He was enjoying the smell of

floor polish and would have quite liked to roll around a bit on the tiles, but this was a serious moment and frivolity would have to wait.

"How peculiar," noted Wilma, looking about. "Where is everyone? The place is empty."

And then it came again. "Help!" sounded the voice. "This way! Thank you!"

"Where's that coming from?" asked Wilma, cocking her head to one side. "I can't quite work it out. Do you think this is part of the entrance exam, Pickle? Detectives sometimes *do* have to save people."

If Pickle could have shrugged, he would have. But he couldn't. Just as he couldn't sit upright in a chair and cross his legs, peel oranges, or conduct an orchestra. Much as he might wish it, he would never be able to do any of these things. It was a burden he had learned to live with.

Wilma set off down the corridor. There was a large notice board to her left. On it was one small note: "Cheese, milk, bread, corn crumbles."

"How strange. It looks like a shopping list. That reminds me. I think I'll eat my biscuits."

Taking the two corn crumbles out of her pinafore pocket, Wilma began to munch. There were rooms off the corridor and as Wilma walked past she pointed them out to Pickle. "'Disguises,'" she read, peering at the brass plate on one door. She stood up on her tiptoes to look in through the window. "It must be a classroom! Look at all those hats! And wigs! What's the next one? 'Creeping and Sneaking.' That sounds good. Oh! Look here. 'Calming Ladies of a Hysterical Persuasion.' How exciting. Let's have a quick peek."

Wilma opened the door into the classroom. "Only one desk," she noted with a small frown. In front of a small blackboard, a wax dummy of a lady in a flouncy blouse was sitting on a display table. The blue-rinsed head was slumped toward the chest and a pair of long arms dangled down. Wilma bent forward to take a closer look. "It's very realistic," she muttered. "Almost spooky."

Wilma reached forward to raise the dummy's head by its chin, but as she touched it, the arms shot upward and a dreadful wailing rang out.

The dummy was screaming! Wilma had activated it!

"Oh no!" Wilma cried as the arms flailed in front of her. The sound was unbearable and Pickle, a sensitive hound who didn't like surprises, took one look at the screaming dummy and ran off to hide behind a pile of books in the corner. "I don't know how to turn it off!" Wilma yelled. "It's gone all hysterical!"

Sticking a finger in one ear, Wilma grabbed a nearby blackboard eraser and threw it at the dummy. It bounced off the waxy quivering chin. But the terrible wailing continued! Then Wilma tried stuffing the dummy into the large trash can to her left, covering it with a bit of curtain and running around the room with it. Not only was it still screaming, but the dummy's windmilling arms were knocking everything on every available surface to the floor. The room looked as if it had been hit by a hurricane.

"This is terrible!" Wilma cried out. "How am I going to stop it? There must be something in here that can help!" She spun around wildly. In the far corner to her right, there was a poster with a picture of a woman sobbing. Above the image were the words: "Hysterical Lady? Needs Calming?" And below: "Remember the three S's! Shake! Shout! Slap!"

"Shake. Shout. Slap," Wilma repeated. "Right then." Taking the dummy—still half stuffed in the bin—by the shoulders, she gave it a quick shake. Then, "Crazy dummy lady!" she yelled over the noise. "Calm down! I said calm down!" Finally, Wilma took her left hand and slapped the dummy firmly across its cheek.

At last, the dummy fell silent, its arms dropping to its side. It had chalk dust on its chin and somehow it had managed to pick up an assortment of ink pens that were now sticking accusingly out of its blue-rinsed hair.

"Thank goodness," Wilma breathed. "Let's hope I don't have to have many lessons in here, eh, Pickle?"

The beagle crept out from his hiding place and trotted nonchalantly to the door, shaking one back leg as he went. It is very important for small dogs to maintain an air of cool at all times. Especially when they have just been hiding in a corner and doing nothing for the last five minutes.

Wilma, still panting, slammed the classroom door shut behind them. "What an awful class that must be!" she said, shaking her head.

"I say!" a voice rang out in the distance. "I wonder if you could help! Hello! Help, please!"

Pickle pricked his ears, went a bit stiff, and pointed his nose firmly in the direction the voice had come from. "You're right," said Wilma with a nod. "It is coming from that way. Let's see who it is!" And off they ran toward the end of the corridor.

The unidentified voice was coming from behind a double set of doors. "Help, please!" it shouted calmly. "This way! Help!" Wilma looked down at Pickle and raised her eyebrows. It was all hugely exciting and if attending the Academy was always going to be like this, then she couldn't wait to join. With a hefty shove, she pushed open the two doors, looked up, and gasped.

"Oh, thank goodness," said the woman hanging

upside down in front of her. "I say, you wouldn't lend a hand, would you? I seem to have gotten myself in an awful mess."

"How did you get all tangled up like that?" asked Wilma, gazing at the figure tethered into a mass of climbing ropes.

"Not quite sure," replied the disheveled lady. "I was trying out some new knots. Anyway. One thing led to another. There's a stepladder over there. You can use that to get up. If I remember correctly, you just have to pull that loose cord at the end of my foot. That should release me."

Wilma ran to fetch the stepladder and then quickly climbed up. She reached for the rope and gave it a sharp tug and the rest of the ropes magically unwrapped themselves and the woman, who had been tied up good and proper, fell suddenly to the floor.

She was dressed in khaki jodhpurs, with a crisp white shirt tucked into the waistband. Her sleeves were rolled up to her elbows and she had brown leather knee boots on. Her hair was a dirty blond, her eyes a flashing green, and she had a dark smudge of something unidentifiable running across one cheek and over her nose. In all, she was the sort of lady that certain gentlemen would say, "If she was tidied up, she'd actually be jolly pretty." But certain gentlemen sometimes don't know what they're talking about and some ladies, however they choose to look, are perfectly lovely just as they are. Remember that.

"Thanks awfully," she said, getting to her feet and dusting herself down. "I'm Kite Lambard. I'm the headmistress here. Who are you?"

"I'm Wilma Tenderfoot," replied the ten-year-old. "I just took the entrance exam."

"Did you really? Golly. Is it Thursday already? I think I've been up there since Monday. Wilma Tenderfoot, eh? Funny sort of name."

"It was pulled out of a hat by Madam Skratch at the Institute for Woeful Children. Quite lucky, really. The orphan before me got Slug Oozely. I used to live at the Institute before I went to work for Mrs. Waldock. Then she got frozen and then I almost got frozen and then I went to work for Theodore P. Goodman instead. I'm his apprentice."

"Oh yes. I think I sent you a letter. Sorry. My memory is shockingly bad. Anyway. Hello. What can I do for you?"

Wilma felt a bit puzzled. "I just took the entrance exam. I had to find the entrance and . . . I did."

Kite blinked and pursed her lips. "Oh, wait. I think I'm supposed to do something official at this point. You'll have to excuse me. You're the first person I've had take the exam. I'm not quite sure what happens next. I'll just check. There's a book somewhere. Got loads of useful stuff in it." She strode over to a desk in the corner and opened some drawers. "Now where did I put it?" she mumbled, having a good rummage. "I think I'm supposed to enroll you or something. But I'm not entirely sure I didn't throw it away . . ."

Wilma shot a quick glance in Pickle's direction. He was looking less than impressed.

"Ah-ha! Panic over!" Kite was waving an important-looking embossed book at them and tapping it with her finger. "Here we are! *How to Enroll a Pupil into the Academy of Detection and Espionage*. Right, then. Let's get on with it." She cleared her throat and began to read. "'Please stand up.' Oh. You're doing that already. Well done. 'You have successfully completed the entrance exam for the Academy of Detection and Espionage.' Seriously—well done. It's jolly difficult. 'Now pass the applicant the textbook *Everything You Will Ever Need to Know About Detection and Espionage*.' Oh. I don't think I was supposed to read that bit out loud. I've got a pile over here. Hang on. Yes! There you go!"

"Thank you," answered Wilma, taking the book from her new headmistress and, opening it to the first page, read out loud:

An Apprentice Detective's Golden Rules

1. Look, listen, and learn.
2. Try to be useful.
3. Always follow orders.
4. If in doubt, stand very still and do nothing.
5. Avoid mucking things up spectacularly.

"Yes," added Kite, "those are quite important. You might want to memorize them. Anyway, back to the ceremony. 'Now give the applicant a leather-bound detective's notebook and an apprentice detective badge and then say something encouraging.' Super. Right. Well, there's your notebook. You can write things in that, I expect. And here's your badge." Kite bent down and pinned a small silver badge to Wilma's pinafore. "Right. Something encouraging . . . Is that your dog?"

"Yes, he is. He's called Pickle," replied Wilma, a bit shell-shocked.

"Good. Though that was sort of a factual question. Encouraging is something a bit different, isn't it? Hang on. I'll have another go. Umm . . . well done. Again. And we're very glad to have you here at the Academy of Detection and Espionage. Super-pleased."

"Where's everyone else?" asked Wilma.

"Everyone else?" replied Kite, eyes widening. "What do you mean?"

"All the other pupils. And teachers."

"Oh!" answered Kite, looking off into the middle distance. "There isn't anyone else. You're the only pupil. I'm the only teacher."

"I see," said Wilma, frowning. "So when do I start taking classes?"

"Classes?" answered Kite, looking a little panicked. "Oh. Well, we don't really do classes. I expect I'll just send you some homework. Like a correspondence course or something like that. It's all mostly in the book. Is there anything specific you'd like to learn?"

Wilma was momentarily silent. She had always been of the opinion that a teacher was someone who was not only in charge but had a vague sense of what she was doing (physics teachers excepted), yet her new headmistress, the one she had just spent the best part of a morning trying to find, seemed to be in such a muddle that it was quite hard not to feel a small stab of disappointment. Still, Wilma had always thought it best to show due respect for her elders and so, very politely, she reached for the luggage tag in her pinafore pocket. "You see," she began, "as well as wanting to learn how to be a proper detective, I'd like to find out where I come from. The thing is I was left at the gates of the Institute for Woeful Children when I was a baby. And this was tied around my wrist," she said, thrusting the tag toward Kite. "It says 'Because they gone.' But I don't know what was because they gone. Or who they were. Or even where they gone. I don't know anything. And then, on top of that, Madam Skratch, who's the matron at the Institute, told me last week that I've got a relative who's still alive. And I'd quite like to find them." She fell quiet once more.

Kite, who seemed a little bewildered, looked down at her new pupil and swallowed. "Golly. That's a puzzle and no mistake. Well!" she added, slapping a hand to her thigh. "I think that sounds like an excellent school project! So why don't you make a start. Send me the occasional report. And then we'll take it from there? Yes?"

"Umm, okay then," replied Wilma, feeling even more baffled.

Kite turned and picked up a pair of leather

goggles from her desk. "Super! Good! Well, that's sorted out then. By the way . . . did you bring the paper bag that smells of pear candies?"

"Oh! I did, yes!" remembered Wilma with a start. "It's here. Would you like it?"

"Yes, please," replied Kite, nodding.

Wilma, who had tucked it up her sleeve earlier, pulled it out. "There you go," she said, grinning. "I wondered why I had to bring it. I expect you're going to teach me some brilliant detective technique or something? You know, to get me started?"

"No, I just like the smell of them," explained Kite, taking a good, deep sniff. "Lovely. Thanks so very much. Well, I suppose that's the end of the induction. Welcome to the Academy. I look forward to your first report. I'd best be off. Got to find a thing. Think I left it there. But then I might not have. Anyway! Good-bye!"

And with that she disappeared through a panel in the wall.

Wilma was stunned. She looked down at the badge on her lapel. It was the school crest with the words "Apprentice Detective" written on it. "Well," she said proudly. "At least I got in, Pickle. And there's no turning back now. Nothing and nobody stops Wilma Tenderfoot!" And she headed for the way out.

What a lovely start to the story. Wilma's done very well and nothing terrible has happened to anyone.

Yet.

"Where is she?" bellowed Inspector Lemone, poking his head around the door to Theodore's study. "I demand to see her! Where's the cleverest girl on Cooper?" Inspector Lemone, a fleshy man with a face shaped like a balloon, wasn't terribly good at inspecting. In many ways, it was slightly baffling that he'd become an Inspector at all, especially in the light of a school report that read quite clearly: "This boy must never become a police officer! NEVER!" Still, grown-ups often end up doing jobs that they clearly have no talent for. Just go and ask any passing adults about their boss. They'll be happy to explain.

Thank goodness then that Inspector Lemone had Theodore P. Goodman to rely on. He couldn't have been more happy that he was working alongside the island's most famous and brilliant detective, principally because it meant he didn't have to do much thinking and could instead concentrate on his real love: eating biscuits. He didn't even have to do any apprehending, as Captain Brock and the 2nd Hawks Brigade were on hand for all manner of capturing and detaining, so in many respects Inspector Lemone wasn't required to do anything at all. Even though he was clearly useless, Inspector Lemone was a loyal companion and would do anything to help Theodore. Not only that, but he was very enthusiastic to encourage young Wilma.

As she saw her portly friend, Wilma beamed. There had been a large fuss made of her since she returned from the Academy and, as a treat, Mr. Goodman and the Inspector were taking her to the Valiant Vaudeville Theatre, somewhere Wilma had always wanted to go. Mrs. Speckle had tried for an hour to tidy Wilma up and make her look respectable, but, after the young girl's socks had fallen down for the fifth time and her plaits had undone themselves for the tenth, she had given up and put a bow tie on Pickle instead. "Well, at least her pinafore is clean!" she said, shaking her head as she presented Wilma to her employer. "That's the best I can do!"

Inspector Lemone, who had a burning fondness for Theodore's housekeeper, always went a bit quiet whenever he was in her presence. Either that or he would blurt out something stupid like: "Do you like eggs? I do."

Mrs. Speckle was, of course, oblivious. She was only interested in getting Mr. Goodman his peppermint tea and corn crumbles. She certainly didn't have time to be paying any attention to slightly silly inspectors or small girls with wayward hair.

Before Wilma joined Theodore's household, the incredibly world-famous detective and the Inspector had been known to travel around

Cooper on a tandem bicycle (much to the slightly overweight Inspector Lemone's dismay). Lemone *hated* riding on the tandem. Still, there was one benefit of being forced to ride on a bicycle made for two—because he always sat at the back, he could just *pretend* to be pedaling.

In order to accommodate the household's new arrivals, Theodore had arranged for a small two-seater trailer to be fitted to the back of his bicycle. This was a substantial thrill for Wilma, who always wanted to follow Mr. Goodman and the Inspector wherever they went.

"Goggles on!" said Wilma as she pulled a matching pair to her own over her beagle's ears. "Off to the theatre, Pickle! Imagine that!"

Pickle did not respond. He just hoped they had good seats.

The Valiant Vaudeville Theatre was in the center of Coop, the island's capital town. The ride there was exhilarating. Bouncing along in the trailer, wind streaming through her hair, Wilma loved every second of it. Because it was a special occasion, Mr. Goodman pulled up at one of Cooper's many Sugarcane Swizzle Dispensing Taps, which were dotted all over the west side of the island. Sugarcane Swizzle was Cooper's finest fizzy drink, made from the crushed pulp of the indigenous Sugarcane Swizzle tree, and as Wilma gulped from the flask that Mr. Goodman had filled, she couldn't think of a finer start to their evening.

Cooper Island was divided into two parts. There was the affluent Farside to the west and the downtrodden Lowside to the east. Having been brought up at the Institute for Woeful Children, Wilma had spent most of her life to date on the dreary Lowside, but now that she was living on the Farside with Mr. Goodman, Wilma was forever amazed at the wondrous differences, like the Sugarcane Swizzle on tap, the air of sunny dispositions, and the splendid buildings, of which the Valiant Vaudeville Theatre was no exception. It was a grand old building, covered with golden friezes of dancing scenes and dramatic moments, topped off with a dark blue dome smothered in silver stars. As Theodore squeezed the brakes of the tandem and came to a stop, Wilma stared up at it with her mouth open. "Wowzees," she whispered in awe.

Inspector Lemone was struggling to adjust his raincoat, which had somehow managed to blow itself over his head during the journey, meaning he was totally unable to see anything. "I am pedaling!" he shouted, not realizing they'd come to a stop. "Golly gosh, Goodman! Are we going uphill?"

"It's all right, Inspector," answered Theodore, undoing his bicycle clips from the bottom of his trousers. "You can dismount now."

"Can I really?" answered the Inspector, one eye finding its way to a buttonhole. "Ah yes. I knew we were here really! Just wanted to keep everyone on their toes and all that!"

As they entered the lobby, Wilma sparkled with excitement. Pictures of artistes appearing on the bill adorned the walls: Loranda Links, the contortionist; Mrs. Wanderlip, ventriloquist; Claiborne Wordette, bird impersonator; Sabbatica, mind reader and woman of mystery; Countess Honey Piccio, the renowned paper tearer; the Great Sylvester, knife thrower and daredevil; Gorgeous Muldoon, the resident comic compère; and in pride of place, in an enormous gilded frame, a picture of the most famous singing and acting diva on Cooper, Cecily Lovely. Wilma gazed upward. They all looked wonderful. She couldn't wait.

"Apple cores!" shouted an usher in a maroon jacket, all gold brocade and buttons. "Get your rotten apple cores!" A tray was hanging around his neck filled with paper cones of rotting fruit.

"What are they for?" asked Wilma, giving the Inspector a nudge.

"For throwing," explained Inspector Lemone. "Oooh. Box of mini corn crumbles. Better get a couple. Do you want one, Goodman? My treat."

"Well, I do love a corn crumble," answered Theodore, mustache twitching at the thought of his favorite biscuits. "And . . ."

But before Theodore could say one more word, Wilma had tugged at his sleeve. He looked down. Her eyes were wide and staring and she was pointing in the direction of the theatre entrance. There, standing in the doorway, was Barbu D'Anvers.

Barbu D'Anvers, arch villain and Mr. Goodman's number one nemesis, was the ghastliest man on Cooper. Like all evil men, he had devoted his life to dodging, dealing, and being utterly diabolical. His purpose—to somehow amass a fortune so gigantic that one day he would be able to buy Cooper Island, rule it with a rod of iron, and open up a center for people who liked built-up shoes (as fashionable attire, not for medicinal purposes—he wasn't short, oh no). Thankfully, he hadn't managed it yet, but that wasn't going to stop him trying.

He was Mr. Goodman's thorniest adversary, and despite coming up against him time and time again, Barbu had always managed to escape the claws of justice. As he stood, the flames of the lamplights burning behind him, Barbu was flanked by his hefty sidekick, Tully, who at that precise moment was struggling with his master's top hat and sizeable black velvet cloak, and his young charge, Janty.

A pang of regret shot through Wilma. It was only a matter of weeks ago that Wilma had encountered this dreadful man for the first time, having previously only read about his dastardly doings in the Cooper press. She couldn't *stand* him. He was rude, foul, and malignant. And, what was worse, he was leading Janty astray. During the Case of the Frozen Hearts, Janty's poor father, Visser Haanstra, had died a horrible death and Theodore, on finding the boy, had offered him his friendship. But Janty, determined to lead a life of crime like his father, had fallen for the devilish promises of D'Anvers and rather than turning his back on a life of wrongdoing, he seemed set to embrace it. Wilma glared at Barbu. As far as she was concerned, it was *all* his fault.

"What's *he* doing here, Mr. Goodman?" whispered Wilma, gripping her mentor's forearm.

"Sadly," replied Theodore with a stern look toward his old enemy, "anybody can come to the theatre. Even if they are rotten to the core. I'm sure he wants to see the show. But we shall keep an eye on him nonetheless. You can never be too sure when Barbu D'Anvers is around."

"Barbu D'Anvers?" asked Inspector Lemone, mouth full of biscuits. "The very rogue! He's the dirtiest sort of skunk! Don't even look at him, Wilma. Just give me a chance to knock him down, Goodman!"

"Well, well," sneered the tiny villain as he swaggered toward them. "If it isn't Theodore P. Goody-Goody-Goodman. And that revolting girl of yours."

"Wilma Tenderfoot," said Janty, curling his lip.

"Yes, I remember you," added Barbu, poking at her pinafore with his cane. "Which is never a good thing. You and I have some unfinished business."

"I'm not afraid of you!" Wilma burst out, pushing past Mr. Goodman's protective hand on her shoulder. "I'm an official apprentice detective now. I've got a badge to prove it!"

Barbu screwed up his face. "Got a badge to prove it?" he mimicked. "Did you hear that, Janty? She's got a baaaaadge. Oooh. I'm terrified!"

Janty laughed cruelly.

"Why don't you pick on someone your own size!" answered Wilma, now almost nose to nose with the villain as Pickle growled protectively. "Oh, hang on a minute," she added with a twinkle, "you are!"

Barbu's jaw tightened. If there was one thing he couldn't bear, it was being told he was small. "Our time will come, Wilma Tenderfoot," snapped the diminutive criminal. "Of that you can be sure." And with a toss of his hair, he swept off toward the auditorium.

Theodore shook his head. "It's not sensible to provoke our enemies, Wilma," he chided. "You must take better care."

"All the same," added Inspector Lemone with a small wink. "That was *quite* good. Anyway, shall we take our seats? We've been standing up for ages. At least five minutes. My legs are killing me."

As the lights went down and the first deep chords struck out from the orchestra pit, Wilma was on the edge of her seat. Pickle was also on the edge of his, but that was because he couldn't quite get the hang of it and every time he tried to sit farther back, the chair folded up on top of him. With the grand curtains across the stage parting to a smattering of unenthusiastic applause, Wilma's heart thumped with excitement and out from the wings stepped a hunched man with a face that looked as if it couldn't quite be bothered.

"That's Gorgeous Muldoon," whispered the Inspector. "He's the compère. That's the fellow who keeps everything moving along."

Wilma nodded and then turned to see that Pickle had almost disappeared down the back of his theatre seat.

"Welcome! Welcome!" Gorgeous began in an almost sleepy drawl. "Welcome to the Valiant Vaudeville Theatre! Prepare to be a-mazed, a-stonished, and even a-fraid! You'll be dazzled. You'll be bewildered! You'll be weeping in your seats! And not just because of the price of the tickets!"

Inspector Lemone laughed. "It's funny," he explained to Wilma, who was extracting Pickle from the mess he'd got himself into, "because it's true. They were quite expensive. Probably explains why they are so few people here. Practically empty. Last time I came it was packed! Mind you, I think I read something about a terrible musical they put on that lost them loads of money. Audiences have been down ever since. They need to do something new. Pep it up! Then they'll have people flooding back in!"

"Shhhh," said a woman in front, turning to give the Inspector a scolding look.

"So," the compère continued, his voice picking up slightly, "ladies and gentlemen! Are you ready to be chilled to the bone? To be baffled and befuddled? Are you ready for a mighty mind-reading mystery? Then please put your hands together and welcome . . . Sabbatica!"

A strange, flute-like instrument piped from the orchestra, filling the auditorium with a haunting air. The lights dimmed to the faintest of glows. Smoke poured across the stage, giving it an aspect so spooky that Wilma, suddenly feeling a little anxious, reached out for Pickle's paw. The flute played on and a dull light fell on the center of the stage. Wilma's eyes followed the dim beam and she could just make out something moving upward through the carpet of smoke. Gasps filled the auditorium as from seemingly nowhere a woman appeared, rising slowly, shrouded in black, her head wrapped in a purple turban. Pickle gave a small whimper. Wilma gripped his paw tighter.

Sabbatica's arms slowly unfolded from inside her voluminous robes, and with the music reaching its peak, her head lifted from her chest until her face, dramatically lit by the single spotlight, was upturned toward the back of the theatre. Her eyes were wild and flaming, her mouth opening and closing as if she was about to speak . . . but then a startled expression crossed her face. Seemingly struggling to breathe, she stumbled forward and with a sudden, desperate clasp of her throat, Sabbatica slumped to the floor.

"This is a very dramatic act," whispered Wilma to Mr. Goodman, sitting on her right. "I wonder what she's going to do next."

But Theodore was already on his feet. "Someone help that woman!" came a cry from the back of the stalls. A scream rang out from somewhere in the wings and Gorgeous Muldoon rushed back onto the stage. Kneeling by Sabbatica's collapsed body, he took her hand in his. "She's dead!" he wailed. "Sabbatica is dead! Oh, help us! Is there a detective in the house?"

"Yes," Wilma shouted back, jumping up and pointing to Mr. Goodman. "And me. I'm the apprentice!"

Do you remember the "Yet" at the end of Chapter Three? Cancel it.

The audience at the Valiant was clearly rattled. Some children were crying, a hairy builder from Hillbottom had fainted, and a wiry-looking woman from Under Whelmed had tried to raise everyone's spirits by singing a spirited version of the Cooper national anthem, only to be told to pipe down by all around her. As Wilma climbed up onto the stage behind Mr. Goodman and the Inspector, a dread chill ran through her. Looking around, she recognized a few faces from the pictures in the foyer: Mrs. Wanderlip, the ventriloquist, and Countess Honey Piccio, the lady who tore paper. Both were in tears, hands clutched to their mouths. Mr. Goodman knelt next to the body and Wilma gulped a little to steel her nerves. She was an apprentice detective now, she thought to herself, giving her new badge a quick glance. This was part of the job, however unpleasant it may be. She would just have to be brave. In fact, according to the Golden Rules, it was her job to be more than brave—she had to be *useful*.

"Shall I chalk around the body, Mr. Goodman?" she asked quietly, wanting to be of help. "I practiced on a dead badger last week."

But Theodore's attentions were elsewhere. A voice was calling from the back of the dress circle. "I say! Goodman!" the voice rang out. "Shall I come down and lend a hand? It's me! Titus Kooks. Got Penbert with me too!"

Theodore shielded his eyes from the overhead lights and looked outward. "That would be splendid, Dr. Kooks!" he shouted back. "Your help would be greatly appreciated."

Dr. Kooks, the island's forensic scientist, and Penbert, his efficient assistant, were on the stage in moments. Penbert, who never liked to do anything unless she was wearing her regulation white coat and clogs, was visibly anxious. "It's not proper procedure otherwise," she explained.

"There's some pink dressing gowns in the wings," suggested Malcolm Poppledore, the pimply props boy, who had wandered onto the stage along with the rest of the shaken actors and crew. "I could get you those, if you like?"

Penbert tightened her lips. It would have to do. "All right," she reluctantly agreed. "They're better than nothing."

"Hello," said Wilma, giving Penbert and Dr. Kooks a nod. "We've met before. When I came to the lab during the Frozen Hearts case. I was dressed like a plumber. So was Pickle. I've got a badge now," she added, tapping the silver crest on her pinafore strap.

The dressing gowns that Malcolm handed over were a vivid pink satin with three-quarter-length arms finished with a fluffy trim. Dr. Kooks took his and pulled it on without a second thought. "Right, then!" he boomed. "Dead body. Let's have a look!"

Sabbatica's body was slumped, face down, center stage. Her purple turban was now askew, and the dark, heavy robes of her costume had fallen across the lower half of her face. As Dr. Kooks peered toward her, one piercing blue eye glared lifelessly back. "Well," he announced after a quick examination, "I can safely say she's dead. In fact, I'd go so far as to say she's very dead."

"Very dead," repeated Inspector Lemone, shaking his head. "Bad business. Write that down, Wilma. Might be important."

"No, don't bother writing that down, Wilma," interjected Theodore with as much patience as he could muster. "I am aware she is dead, Dr. Kooks, but can you tell me why or how?"

Dr. Kooks blinked, tapped his considerable belly with his fingers, and blew some air out through his lips. "No," he finally replied. "No. I can't."

"It might have been a heart attack," muttered Wilma, licking the end of her pencil and reaching for her notebook. "Collapsing like that with no warning." She turned to a scowling Gorgeous

Muldoon. "Did she eat a lot of cheese? Late at night? Don't worry. I am an apprentice detective." She pointed to her badge.

"Cheese does not cause heart attacks, Wilma," corrected Theodore, standing up from the body. "Unless eaten in massive quantities. In any event, I don't think that was the cause of death. And stop asking people questions. I think it's best if you just stand there and observe. I shall deal with this."

Wilma tried her best not to look too disappointed, as she was itching to write something in her brand-new official detective's notebook, but now that she was in Mr. Goodman's employ it was best to do as she was told. Most of the time. Instead, Wilma flicked through her notebook and read some of the articles that she had transferred there from her Clue Ring. There was the one about the Case of the Dropped H and the two-page picture special of the Case of the Moldy Knees, but there was nothing about what to do when a mind reader expires in mysterious circumstances. Perhaps the detective's top tips that she'd written in the front might help her. "Number six . . ."

she muttered, tapping the relevant page with her pencil, "always write things down."

No one was paying any attention to her, of course, but it did make her feel a little bit more useful and apprentice-ish.

Theodore, with a small twitch of his mustache, bent close to the Inspector for a quiet word. "Scan the audience for Barbu D'Anvers. Quietly, though. Interested to know where the fellow is."

"Think it was him, Goodman?" he whispered, one eye winking. "Wouldn't be in the least bit surprised."

"Hang on!" Penbert called out suddenly as she crouched next to the body. "There's something on the floor. Looks as if it's dripped out of her mouth."

Everyone turned to look. Penbert, very carefully, pulled back Sabbatica's heavy costume. Her face was as white as lilies, but around her mouth, at the corners and on her lips, there was a strange yellowish foam. "Does anyone have some gloves I can borrow?" she asked, looking over her shoulder.

"I've got a pair of rubber gloves," answered Malcolm Poppledore.

"I have some lace ones," offered the paper-tearing Countess.

"Rubber, please," answered Penbert, still staring at the bubbling foam. Malcolm stepped forward and passed her the gloves.

"Pooh," he said, waving a hand in front of his nose as he did so. "Something smells terrible!"

"It's the foam," explained Penbert, snapping on a glove and sticking a finger into it. "It's positively putrid. This is definitely not a heart attack," she added, casting a glance up at Theodore. "In fact, if I was to make an assumption, which I'm not used to and, strictly speaking, is against every scientific protocol and I haven't made anything near to a detailed report or any sort of proper analysis, let alone logged it, bagged it, OR tagged it—"

"Do get on with it, Penbert!" roared Dr Kooks.

"Well," said Penbert, pushing her thick glasses very firmly up her nose. "I think she's been poisoned!"

A gasp rang out around the auditorium. "Poisoned!" cried a deep, trembling voice from the wings. "Dear Sabbatica poisoned?" Wilma spun around. "Say it isn't so!"

A woman wafted onto the stage. Her frame was delicate, like a bird's, but her presence was magnificent, like a lion's. A small ripple of applause broke out in the audience. "Thank you, thank you," the woman acknowledged with a weak wave of her hand. "But please! Save your applause for happier times! Oh, Sabbatica! Oh!"

And with that she too drifted to the floor—in a precise heap. The audience gasped again.

"Not her as well!" yelled Wilma, rushing over.

"It's all right," said a scrappy-looking girl in spectacles, hurrying to the woman's side. "Miss Lovely is often prone to swooning. She has a very fragile constitution."

"Ooooh," whispered Inspector Lemone, straightening his waistcoat. "That's Cecily Lovely. I've got all her records. And I've seen all her plays. Wonder if she'd like a corn crumble?"

"Not now, Inspector," replied Theodore, rushing to help the fallen diva to her feet. "Madam, can I be of assistance?"

"Scraps!" mumbled the great actress, weakly reaching for her assistant. "My smelling salts . . . dressing room table . . . I must . . . oh!" And with that she faded again, a little more dramatically, and this time with her face better turned to the light, because as all ladies of a certain age know, if you're going to faint, make sure you show off your best side as you do it.

"I'll fetch her smelling salts," said Scraps, her bony legs rattling inside her shoes. "She needs air. Waft something at her, would you?" she added, looking at Wilma anxiously. Sometimes, people in the same boat are drawn toward one another and, as she stared at Scraps in her raggedy patch-work dress and with her limp brown hair a mess of tangles, Wilma realized that here was someone hard at it, just like her.

Wilma nodded. "Don't worry," she said softly. "I'll waft my notebook at her. At least that way I'll get to use it today."

"Thank you." Scraps smiled weakly. "I'd better hurry."

"Sabbatica's dead and Cecily still has to be the

center of attention," grumbled Loranda Links, the contortionist, pushing past Wilma as she walked toward the wings.

"I hope you're not going anywhere, Miss Links," said Theodore quickly. "I'm afraid under the circumstances I am going to have to ask everyone who works here not to leave the theatre for the time being. Given that we're dealing with a poison," Theodore added, turning to the Inspector, "I think we can assume it would have been administered before the performance. In light of that, you can allow the audience to leave, Inspector. Oh, and any sighting of our friend?"

The Inspector shook his head. "He was in that box to the right. Saw him when we sat down. But he's not there now. Danged suspicious if you ask me!"

Theodore looked up toward the empty box, momentarily lost in thought. Wilma watched him and, because she should be trying to learn practical things during her apprenticeship, she went and stood next to him and stared up too.

"Got them!" called out Scraps, returning speedily from the backstage area.

Her hands, Wilma noted, were gloved: cotton gloves, once obviously white but now a grubby gray. "Everyone's got gloves," she reflected, remembering that a detective's job was to notice as many things as possible. "Must be a theatre thing."

As Scraps ran, she held out a tiny green bottle of smelling salts, but just as she approached her mistress, her gangly legs caught in a pulley rope and she fell headfirst into a piece of painted scenery. The bottle of smelling salts dropped to the stage and smashed open, sending the small odorous crystals scattering everywhere.

"Oh no," she cried, scrabbling frantically to try to save something. "Miss Lovely's salts! Now what am I going to do? I'll be in terrible trouble. Nothing rouses her except these!"

If there was one thing Wilma believed in, it was lending a hand to someone who needed it, and seeing the poor girl desperate before her, Wilma knew what she could do. "You can use my dog if you like," she said, putting a hand on Scraps's bony shoulder.

"Your dog?" replied Scraps, tears in her eyes as she looked up. "What good will a dog do?"

"He's got terrible breath. Honestly. It would raise the dead. I'll get him to breathe on your mistress. She'll be awake in no time." Turning to Pickle, who had been enjoying chewing an old wig he'd found on a table, Wilma picked him up, placed his snout as close to Miss Lovely's nose as she could, and said, "Go on, Pickle, yawn!"

The beagle, who was tired anyway, needed no further encouragement. His mouth opened to a gape, out lolled his tongue, and with eyes clamped shut, Pickle let a deep gust of dog breath roll onto the diva's face.

"Ohhhh!" she screamed, her eyes popping open. "Ohh, that smell! It's like a thousand dead things blended into one vile stench! Scraps! Get this hound off me! Scraps!"

"I'm here, Miss Lovely," said the set-upon dresser, stepping forward to take her mistress's hand. "Thank you," she mouthed silently to Wilma.

"Take me to my dressing room," warbled the

actress, lifting a limp wrist to her forehead. "I am on the verge of an emotional eclipse. Excuse me. I must retire. Adieu. Oh, and please, Mr. Goodman," she added, grabbing Theodore suddenly by the arm. "Find whoever committed this *unspeakable* act and toss them from the theatre!"

And with that she limped offstage, but not before she'd managed three bows to the audience.

Actors, eh? Pfffft.

Baron von Worms, the manager of the Valiant Vaudeville Theatre, was pacing. His long silk coat was flapping and his hand was running anxiously through his considerable hair, so voluminous it looked like the top swirl of an ice-cream cone. "This could ruin me, Goodman!" he whined, slumping himself into the chair behind his desk. "The theatre is already on the verge of bankruptcy! Ever since we put on *Swamp!* We lost so much money—we've been in trouble ever since!"

"*Swamp?*" asked Wilma, looking puzzled.

"The musical I was telling you about," answered

Inspector Lemone, before adding with a whisper, "It stank."

"Now this!" continued the Baron, his head falling into his hands. "And tonight of all nights. I had a potential investor in the audience. He's due in to see me at any moment! He's hardly going to be interested anymore is he? Mind reader poisoned live in front of an audience! Thank goodness the papers weren't in. One more bad review and we're done for!"

Wilma looked around her. Being an apprentice, as many grown-ups will tell you, mostly involves keeping quiet and doing boring things like fetching sandwiches or polishing magnifying glasses, but Wilma, while she wasn't allowed to ask questions or do much deducting or contemplating, was allowed to keep her eyes peeled for things like clues and a new thing that Mr. Goodman had called "anomalies." These were things that seemed out of place or didn't add up. Besides, now she had the Golden Rules to adhere to, it was important that she try to make herself as useful as possible.

Wilma had never been in a theatre manager's office before, so it was quite difficult at first glance to tell if anything was out of place. There were heaps of scripts, a couple of feather boas, a large owl costume, a xylophone, a sequined dress hanging on a hat stand, a large box of grease-paints, and a small bucket and spade.

"Bucket and spade?" Wilma muttered to herself as the Baron rattled on in the background. "Perhaps that's an omen-knee?" She wandered over and picked up the bucket. It smelled salty, like the sea, and there was a small piece of seaweed at the bottom.

"What are you doing?" asked the Baron, snatching it back suddenly.

"Just looking for omen-knees. I'm an apprentice detective," replied Wilma, a little startled, slipping a small piece of seaweed into her pinafore pocket.

"Anomalies, Wilma," corrected Theodore, raising his eyebrows at her. "Now just stand over there. If I want you to do something, I promise I shall ask you."

"Yes, Mr. Goodman." Wilma shrugged. It was quite frustrating not really being able to do anything, but she was allowed to look, listen, and learn. Which was better than nothing. Still, she thought, eyeing the bucket, it was quite odd. The other things looked like they might belong in a theatre, but the bucket didn't. Perhaps she'd think about it again later.

"Did Sabbatica have any enemies, Baron?" asked the great detective, pulling his pipe from his pocket. "That's not to say that it can't be accidental, of course. Was she taking any strange herbal remedies, for instance? Had she eaten anything peculiar?"

"In my textbook from the Academy of Detection and Espionage," piped up Wilma, reaching into her pinafore pocket, "there's a whole chapter on poisonings. 'When poison is involved, it's generally administered by someone with a grudge or a need for secrecy or revenge.' That's what it says. And there's a list of poisons. And—"

"Wilma," said Theodore firmly. "Please be quiet. Let the Baron answer."

Baron von Worms shook his head. "I have no idea! She seemed to be reasonably popular. But then, it is hard to tell. They all call each other darling. So there's no way of knowing. There was a bit of tension between her and Cecily. Sabbatica was younger, you see. And Cecily has started to get wrinkles. I'm sure it's nothing."

"No," replied Theodore, packing his pipe with some rosemary tobacco. "Everything is useful." The great detective turned to look at his apprentice. "Did you write that bit down? If you didn't, you might want to."

Wilma's eyes widened. Something official at last! She took out her pencil and notebook and made a note. "I could ask Scraps more about that."

Theodore twitched his mustache in thought. "All right then, later," he said after a moment. "Seeing as you are both girls. She might feel happier talking to you. But I don't want you letting slip anything that you shouldn't, Wilma. Remember the top tips—a detective always saves what he's thinking till last."

"And the Golden Rules, Mr. Goodman," said

Wilma with a nod, keen to show her employer she was advancing. "The one about being useful! I can do that while I ask the questions."

Wilma was practically beside herself. Not only had she gotten to write down something that could turn out to be incredibly important, but she was also going to be allowed to do some investigating. She made a mental note to consult the relevant chapter in her textbook. As well as proving she could be useful, it was vital to show her mentor that she'd been listening and thereby learning. Like a good apprentice. It was very important that she should proceed properly, just like Mr. Goodman.

Suddenly there was a sharp rap on the door and Malcolm Poppledore, the props boy, stuck his head into the room. "Gentleman to see you, Mr. von Worms," he said with a sniff.

"Baron von Worms, Malcolm, *Baron,*" replied the exasperated manager, rolling his eyes. "Show him in, please. Mr. Goodman, that'll be my investor. I'll have to ask you to leave. I really can't think of anything further to help. But if I do I'll let you know."

"Baron!" boomed a voice from the doorway. Everyone turned to look. "What a perfectly spectacular evening!" It was Barbu D'Anvers, closely followed by Tully and Janty.

"Oh no, not him," mumbled the Inspector, reaching for the last corn crumble in his box.

"Mr. Goodman," acknowledged the diminutive villain with an ironic bow. "We meet again! And so soon! Aren't I the lucky one?"

"Let's go, Wilma, Inspector," said the detective, ignoring him. "And take care, Barbu. I shall be keeping a close eye on things here. Mark my words."

Wilma leaned in toward Janty, who glared back at her. "You'll come to no good if you stick with him, you know," she hissed as Theodore made his way toward the door.

"I'm glad," sneered the boy in return. "I like being no good. It's fun."

Wilma shook her head disapprovingly. "Come on, Pickle," she added, gesturing to her beagle. "There is a sudden bad smell in this room. And for once it's not you."

And with that Wilma, Pickle, the Inspector, and the great detective left.

Barbu glared at the just-shut door and blew a loud raspberry. "Is it possible to despise a man more? No! It isn't! How can he stand being that dull? I mean, honestly?!"

"I'm so sorry about this evening, Mr. D'Anvers." The Baron squirmed, rubbing his hands together. "Most unfortunate. But then, that's theatre! You never know what's going to happen! Ha-ha-ha. All the same. It's not what I would have liked. And such a shame! You didn't get to see Mrs. Wanderlip! Wonderful ventriloquist! And the Countess! Her paper tearing is second to none! Believe me, there's not a greater——"

"That will do," snapped Barbu, holding a hand up. "I'm not really interested in your pathetic acts. But someone dying onstage . . . now that's an opportunity. Everyone will want to come here. I can see it now. The stage of death! There's a killing to be made! Pardon the expression. So, Baron, I am pleased to be able to tell you that I *will* be making an investment."

The Baron's face lit up, his mouth gaped, and for a second he was so stunned he was unable to speak. Instead a small squeak squeezed out from the back of his throat. "Y-you are?" he stuttered eventually. "Actually going to give me money? I . . . I don't know what to say! Except thank you! Thank you, Mr. D'Anvers! You won't regret this! I'll be able to fix the leak in the ceiling! Repaint the scenery! Get some new props!"

Baron von Worms shot from his chair, arms outstretched, ready to hug his investor. He had almost reached Barbu when Tully, the villain's henchman, pulled him back by the scruff of his collar.

"I don't do cuddles," said Barbu, recoiling. "And a little quicker next time if you please, Tully. He almost made contact."

"Yes, Mr. Barbu," said the stupid sidekick, scratching the side of his nose.

"Oh!" said the Baron, a little startled. "Well, that's all right! Ha-ha! We don't need to hug! But it's fantastic news! Amazing! I'm the luckiest manager alive! Having Barbu D'Anvers as the Theatre Angel!"

"Sorry," said Barbu, frowning. "An *angel*? Me?"

"Yes!" The Baron grinned. "An angel! That's what we call people who give money to theatrical productions!"

"My mother will be turning in her grave," replied Barbu, one eyebrow arching. "Although you might not think me so heavenly when you read my terms. Janty! Give him the contract!"

The young boy pushed a dark curl out of his eyes and reached into his trouser pocket. "Here you are, Mr. von Worms," he said, handing over a folded piece of paper.

"Baron. Baron von . . ." began the manager, but catching Barbu's unimpressed eye he cleared his throat and let it go. Instead he took the contract and read. His face, which moments before had been so filled with relief and gratitude, fell. "B-but . . ." he stuttered, frowning as he read, "this can't be! In exchange for your initial investment, it says here you want ninety-nine percent of all ticket sales going forward. But that's not possible!"

"Oh, it's entirely possible, *Mr.* von Worms,"

replied Barbu, smirking. "Either you accept my terms or you get no money. And, according to my sources, who tell me you've tried every investor on Cooper and failed, I am your one hope."

The Baron slumped.

"Just as I thought." Barbu smirked. "So you *will* sign my contract. And what's more, Goodman isn't the only one who wants to keep a close eye on things. I intend to move myself here immediately. This is now my office. And I'd be grateful if you'd get out of it. See the gentleman to the door, would you, Tully?"

"But I . . . but . . ." spluttered the Baron as he was bundled away.

"Right, then!" sighed Barbu, taking a quick look about him. "Let's make some money. Hmm. Is that an owl costume? Ooh . . . sequins."

"Now then, Wilma. I have a job for you," Mr. Goodman announced.

Wilma was sitting by the fire in Theodore's study. Pickle was in the armchair opposite. Between them there was a small round table on top of which sat a Lantha board. (Lantha, for those of you not paying attention, is the favorite board game of all Cooperans. You can play it if you like—the board and rules are at the end of the book.) They had been trying to play since getting up that morning but, after Pickle had knocked everything to the floor for the third time, it had all ground to a halt.

"I give up. That's the last time I'm playing a board game with you, Pickle," Wilma said, bending down to retrieve the scattered pieces. "And I'm not entirely convinced that you haven't been cheating either."

Pickle looked sheepish. He *had* been cheating.

Theodore leaned back into his chair and put his thumbs in his waistcoat pockets. "I'd like you to make me a Clue Board for this case."

Wilma's mouth dropped open. This was by far the most important job she had been given during her apprenticeship to date. She had made her own Clue Board during the Case of the Frozen Hearts, but it hadn't been an official one, so getting to make one for Mr. Goodman was an incredible honor.

"Now, at present we don't know whether the poison was taken by accident or whether it was administered with foul intent. If it was the act of an island Criminal Element, then it is highly likely that it was someone who works at the theatre. That's not to say that it couldn't have been administered by a member of the audience, of course—Barbu D'Anvers was present—but we should start by eliminating the people closest to the victim. Any one of them could have administered the poison before the performance. Inspector Lemone will give you the names of everyone who was there," Theodore added, "when he's finished eating biscuits."

"Just found a stray one in my pocket, Goodman," spluttered the Inspector, trying to look innocent.

"You should find a chapter in your textbook about Clue Boards to remind you how to make one, so read that first. And then, when you're done, perhaps you can give us a small presentation? We can call it a Case Review. Say in an hour, after lunch? If your Clue Board is clear enough, then I might let you transfer everything onto my board in the study. And then we can head over to the theatre. Time is of the essence. How does that sound?"

Wilma nodded with some enthusiasm. "Thank you, Mr. Goodman." She beamed. "I'll get on it right away!"

Well, this was a privilege! Jam-packed with a surge of get-up-and-go, Wilma ran off to her room, Pickle in tow, and opened her textbook. "Right, then," she said, running a forefinger down the list of chapter headings. "Clue Boards . . . Clue Boards . . . Hang on. There's a chapter in here called 'Lost Relatives and How to Find Out About Them'! She quickly flicked to the relevant page.

Relatives can be slippery and easily lost. The first thing you need to establish is whether they are lost or whether they have died in terribly sad circumstances. If they ARE lost, then you will need to find out who the last person to have contact with them was. Perhaps it was the milkman. Or a gentleman who came about the drains.

Wilma stopped reading. "I'll just make a note of that," she mumbled, reaching for her notebook. "No time to think more about it now, though. I have to get on with the Clue Board."

She scanned the index pages quickly. "Capers

of a criminal nature, page twenty-two; cast-iron alibis, page thirty-four; clapped-out excuses, page seventy-two; Clue Boards, page sixty-seven!"

Clue Boards are crucial to any case. They are quick, visual reminders for all detectives and serve to keep track of what's happened, to whom, why, when, and how. A Clue Board should be clear and precise. Do not cover it with clutter or anything that is not important to the case. You would not, for example, pin a dry-cleaning ticket to a Clue Board. Nor would you decorate it with tinsel or pictures of friends and family making stupid faces. A Clue Board is not for fun. A Clue Board is a serious detecting tool.

Clue Boards can vary in size. Some can even vary in shape. But all Clue Boards should contain the following information:

1. The nature of the crime. What has happened?
2. The victim. To whom did it happen?

3. A map or picture of where the crime took place. Preferably with arrows. These will help focus attention and can give a Board a dramatic look. Which is lovely.

4. A list of the suspects, along with their pictures, for quick identification.

5. Motives. Crimes generally happen for a reason. Why? And who benefits?

6. Any forensic results. Especially knotty ones are excellent. Complicated scientific data will bamboozle suspects and, more importantly, make you look good.

7. General clues, contemplations, and deductions.

8. Connections between suspects, maps, clues, motives, science, and victims should be made using string and pins. Blue string is best.

When you have made your Clue Board, remember to place it in a prime position for easy viewing. Putting it in a closet under the stairs or halfway up a tree is going to be no good to anyone, so pick an open spot with plenty of light.

"First things first then, Pickle," Wilma announced, thumping the book closed and leaping off her bed. "We need to find something to make the board out of and some blue string!

"Mrs. Speckle!" Wilma panted, running down the stairs and into the kitchen. "Mr. Goodman has asked me to make a Clue Board and I was wondering if——"

"No time!" barked Mrs. Speckle, who was rolling out a piece of pastry to go over a pie. "There's this to finish, a pudding to bake, and, what's more, my Wellingtons are worn through! I need to knit myself some new ones! You'll have to find something on your own!"

Wilma, who was small but very determined, knew she needed to tread carefully. "Don't suppose you've got any blue string then?" she asked, twisting the bottom of her pinafore.

"No, I do not!" snapped Mrs. Speckle, pushing up the double bobble hats that had slumped down over her eyes. "Blue string indeed. Off with you! I'm up to my eyes in kidneys and puffy toppings! I can't be bothered with small girls and beagles and their incessant questions. Try in the attic! That's packed with rubbish!"

Pickle, as we all know, is no slouch. And as the irascible housekeeper sent them packing he had the wherewithal to very quietly pick up a loose thread that was hanging from the back of Mrs. Speckle's battered blue Wellington. As he trotted away, the boot on Mrs. Speckle's left foot slowly began to unravel and, by the time he and Wilma had gotten themselves to the attic door, Pickle had a considerable length of loose wool hanging from his mouth and Mrs. Speckle was staring down at her woolen sock wondering where her boot had gone.

"Oh!" said Wilma, bending down to roll the length of wool into a ball. "Where did you get this? This will be perfect for our Clue Board."

Pickle looked the other way. After all, Wilma didn't need to know EVERYTHING.

The attic was a dusty mess. Filled with boxes and rolled-up rugs, it looked as if someone had tipped a house upside down and shaken the contents into it. There were books, photograph albums, lamp shades, teacups, cake tins, bicycle saddles, large terrible paintings, tablecloths, and, much to Pickle's alarm, a stuffed dog on wheels. At first sight, there didn't seem to be anything that Wilma might be able to use, but she wasn't about to be deterred that easily.

"Mr. Goodman always says," she explained to Pickle as she pushed aside a heap of blankets, "that a good detective should be able to think not just in a straightforward way, but in an upside-down, roundabout way as well. He gives it a proper phrase. It's called 'thinking outside of the box.' So let's try it. There's nothing here that looks as if we can use it, but, thinking in a wonky way, that large terrible painting over there wouldn't be missed by anyone. Who wants a picture of a bunch of dogs playing poker? Nobody."

Pickle shook his head in agreement.

"So if we take that and paint it white, then we'll have ourselves a Clue Board. And that, Pickle, is the best cockeyed thought I expect I'll have today."

Theodore had one eye on his fob watch. It was a few seconds to his post-lunch peppermint tea and corn crumbles, and with Inspector Lemone quietly dozing on the chaise longue, there was a fighting chance that, for once, he might get to the biscuits first.

The door to his study flew open.

"Mr. Goodman!" announced Wilma, splattered with paint. "I have completed the Clue Board. Bring it in, Pickle!"

Pickle, covered with paint from nose to tail, had a rope in his mouth. Behind him the Clue Board was balanced precariously on the back of the stuffed dog on wheels.

Theodore, sensing that everything was teetering on the edge of disaster, got up. "Let me help you with that," he said, rushing over to take hold of the board. "Quite large, isn't it? Where do you want it to go, Wilma? It's quite heavy too . . . in fact . . ."

"Peppermint tea and corn crumbles, Mr. Goodman!" rattled Mrs. Speckle, marching in behind them.

"Corn crumbles?" mumbled the Inspector, opening an eye.

"I'll just put them here," she added, slamming her tray down on a side table. "They're right next to you, Inspector. Can't stop. Only got one Wellington." And with that she marched straight back out again.

Theodore peered out from behind the Clue Board. The biscuits were already gone. "Would it be too much to ask that occasionally you might wait for me to take one before eating all the corn crumbles, Inspector?"

"Corn crumbles gone?" asked the Inspector, sitting up and swallowing rapidly. "So they have. Who did that then?"

"Over here, please, Mr. Goodman," directed Wilma, pointing toward an easel that she had placed in the corner of the room next to the window. "I'm ready for the Case Review now. Pickle, can I have the stick, please?"

Wilma's Clue Board was a mass of wool, arrows, and scraps of paper. Unable to find proper pictures of any of her suspects, she had resorted to making collage faces from old pictures in magazines. She had cut eyes out here and chins out there. Odd noses were glued onto skewed mouths and, in at least one picture, she had used animal ears instead of human ones.

"This case started," Wilma began as Theodore sat down and picked up his cup of peppermint tea, "when Sabbatica"—she pointed her stick toward a face with one large eye—"was killed by a suspicious substance that was almost certainly a poison." She moved her stick along a piece of blue wool to a hand-drawn picture of a bottle with a skull and crossbones on it. "This took place at the Valiant Vaudeville Theatre. I couldn't find a picture of it, so I've used this drawing of a cowshed instead. She may have been poisoned by accident, so I have drawn a picture of a moldy fish. But she may have also been poisoned quite deliberately. So far the top suspects are everyone who was supposed to appear onstage that night." She ran her stick along a long line of disfigured faces. "But it also could have been anyone who worked at the theatre. There's the prop boy, Malcolm Poppledore; Mrs. Grumbletubs, the laundry mistress—I ran out of eyes, but I'm assuming she has some in real life; and her son, Geoffrey, who carries things around. Obviously it might also have been anyone in the audience. I have stuck up a picture of Barbu D'Anvers because he's the most likely."

"I don't recall D'Anvers having goofy teeth and a pair of thick spectacles . . ." Inspector Lemone frowned, rubbing his chin.

"Never mind that now," battled on Wilma, "because, last but not least, we must also include the manager himself, Baron von Worms. And this bucket. With some seaweed in it."

"Bucket and seaweed?" asked Theodore, trying not to smile too much.

"Yes," said Wilma in a very serious manner, "it's almost definitely an omen-knee."

"Anomaly, Wilma," corrected Theodore. "Say it again. An-omo-lee."

"An-omo-lee," repeated Wilma slowly.

"So in your professional opinion, Wilma," the great detective continued, raising his chin a little, "who do you think is the culprit? Remember we need to think about not only who, but how and why. Who had the motive, Wilma? Something against Sabbatica?"

Wilma mustered up her most serious face to date. This, she realized, would be a good time to tap her stick on the Clue Board a bit more. In an official capacity. So she did. Then pursing her lips and knotting her eyebrows, she turned to her mentor. "To conclude, Mr. Goodman," she pronounced with some importance, "and thinking wonkily, it could be anyone."

"That is certainly very . . . wonky," replied Theodore with a small nod. "Well, for a first attempt, it's not that bad, Wilma. You've grasped the basics. It's a bit busy and we'll have to change . . . well . . . all of it, but not bad."

"And I didn't know Cecily Lovely had cat's ears," said the Inspector, taking a closer look at the Clue Board."

"Oh yes," answered Wilma, giving the Clue Board its firmest tap yet. "Ohhh yes."

And we're off.

"**U**gh," said Barbu D'Anvers with a grimace. Standing at the window of his office in the Valiant Vaudeville Theatre, he was staring down into the street. "That ghastly detective is back with his idiot Inspector and that revolting child. Is there any way we can stop them? Can't I ban them from coming in or something?"

"Probably not, master," answered Janty, who was busy painting a large sign that read "STAGE OF DEATH!" "Besides, having a detective snooping around will remind everyone that someone's died. It'll be good for business."

Barbu turned and smirked at his young charge. "Well, well," he said, twirling his cane. "You do surprise me. Thinking like a proper villain already. You're right. Having him here WILL be good for business. In fact, we must keep him here for as long as possible. Hamper their investigations, Janty. After all, we don't want him to *solve* the case. Let's make things difficult for them. That way, we get to remind people that the theatre has had a grisly death AND that Theodore P. Goodman is utterly hopeless!"

He wandered over to the sign and stared at it. "Bit more blood there, I think," he commented, pointing with his cane.

"Today, Wilma," began Theodore as they strode through the theatre doors into the lobby, "we shall begin the more formal side of our investigation. Let's familiarize ourselves with the backstage areas of the theatre, and I think that chat with young Scraps might be something you could concentrate on. But I want you to tread carefully. Let's practice. We'll pretend I'm Scraps and you're going to ask me some questions. Off you go."

Wilma blinked, frowned, then, scrunching her nose up, said, "Hello, Scraps. Did Cecily Lovely kill Sabbatica?"

"Now," the great detective corrected gently, "you see, that's what I would call a little heavy-handed. Subtlety is the key, Wilma. Start informally. Find out how long she's been working for Cecily. What her chores are. This way you will establish trust. Once you have her trust, you can ask more probing questions. Questions about Cecily, her personality, her likes and dislikes."

"And whether she killed Sabbatica," added Wilma, nodding.

Theodore looked down at his very young apprentice. "Hmmm," he mumbled. "Perhaps this isn't such a good idea. Let's put you on backstage duties instead. The midday show is due to start soon. Stay in the wings, Wilma. Get a sense for the lay of the land."

Wilma looked blank. Pickle looked blanker.

"You do understand what 'lay of the land' means, don't you?"

"Not really, Mr. Goodman," replied Wilma, rubbing her cheek. "Is it one of those special detective phrases, like thinking wonkily out of boxes?"

"Sort of," answered Theodore patiently. "It means to assess the area you're in. Get to know it. Become familiar with exits and passageways. That sort of thing. Do you think you can do that?"

Wilma nodded. Being a detective's apprentice was proving to be quite hard work. And involved lots of strange phrases. But even though she was small, Wilma was very determined, so she would try her best, follow orders like she was supposed to, and hope that she didn't muck things up too spectacularly.

"Good. You and Pickle head off there then, and the Inspector and I will go and make inquiries as to whether Sabbatica had eaten anything she shouldn't. Then I need to see the Baron. I want to find out more about the financial difficulties the theatre is in. May not be connected to what happened, but we can never be too careful."

The backstage area of the Valiant Vaudeville Theatre was buzzing with activity. As Wilma made her way into the wings, she could hear the audience coming into the auditorium on the other side of the safety curtain. There was an air of excitement. Ushers were shouting at people to sit in the right seats, people were calling out for rotten apple-core cones, and somewhere, over it all, there was one lone child wailing.

Onstage, Malcolm Poppledore was ticking things off his props list and running around yelling every time he couldn't find something. A small, red-faced woman was carrying great piles of costumes and hanging them in dressing areas in the wings lit with tiny lanterns.

"Mrs. Grumbletubs!" shouted Malcolm, spotting her. "You haven't seen Eric Ohio's cowboy hat, have you?"

The costume mistress shouted back over her shoulder, "Laundry room. Wringer. On top."

"Eric Ohio?" asked Wilma, casting a look down at Pickle. "Who's that? His name's not on our suspect list."

"And neither should it be," rattled Malcolm as he ran past. "He's Mrs. Wanderlip's ventriloquist dummy. Geoffrey!" he shouted to a sullen-looking boy watering a small potted plant in the wings. "Move that scenery for me, would you? Excuse me, please! House opens in five! In five, everyone!"

Wilma looked over at Geoffrey. He was slightly tubby and was wearing a threadbare sweater that was tucked into a pair of trousers that were slightly too short for him. He had a belt around his waist from which hung a variety of hooks and wrenches and a pair of battered leather gloves. He was also wearing one red shoe and one blue shoe, which struck Wilma as being a little odd. "He doesn't look very happy, does he, Pickle? Perhaps I'd better write that down. I should also write down where all the exits are, like Mr. Goodman told me. Mind you, it's quite hard to work it out. It's dark back here. Be careful, Pickle, there are ropes everywhere. So Malcolm just walked off over there," she added, pointing with the end of her pencil. "That's to the right of the stage."

"No, that's stage left," mumbled Geoffrey, who was dragging a large piece of painted canvas toward them.

Wilma, readying her pencil, followed Geoffrey's eye line. "But it's over there." Wilma pointed again, toward the door. "That's the right."

"Yes." Geoffrey nodded. "But right is stage left. And left is stage right."

"Hang on a minute," said Wilma, putting one hand on her hip. "Is this some sort of hocus-pocus? How can left be right and right be left? Which one is which?"

"Well, to the right is left," said Geoffrey. "And to the left is right. And upstage is the downstage. And downstage is the upstage. It's easy when you know how," he added, before wandering off.

"Well, this complicates everything," said Wilma, looking both left and right. "Upstage, downstage, stage left—I don't know whether I'm coming or going. What's wrong with just saying over there and leaving it at that? And I tell you something else, Pickle. That boy wanted to confuse me. You know what that means . . ."

Pickle snorted.

"That he may be sneaky. I'll make a note. And contemplate that later. Oh! This lay-of-the-land business is harder than it looks. It's making my head spin." Wilma heaved a small sigh and chewed her lip. "Maybe we should go and see Scraps," she wondered, standing back to avoid a large sandbag that was being lowered from a rope above her. "I expect Mr. Goodman would be very pleased if I managed to solve this case in one probing. What do you think, Pickle?"

The beagle, sensing that this was one of those moments where the less he had to do with something, the better, lay on his back and waved his legs in the air.

"Snooping about?" said a voice behind them. Wilma spun around.

"Not snooping, thank you, Janty," she replied with a sniff. "I am conducting official detective business."

The boy kicked at a rope with the end of his

foot, his dark mop of hair falling forward into his eyes. "But you're not an official detective, are you? In fact, from where I'm standing, you're nothing at all."

Wilma's lips tightened. Having been at the Institute for Woeful Children for ten years, she knew full well when someone was trying to annoy her. Standing a little taller and straighter, she matched him head-on. "I'm an apprentice. I'm learning how to be a detective. Rather like how you're learning to be rotten to the core. One of us is going to achieve something in life. One of us is not."

Janty glared at Wilma through his heavy bangs. "My master owns this theatre. Soon he'll own everything. And, when he does, I shall have everything and you'll achieve nothing. I shall see to it."

"Stealing and double dealing is no achievement, Janty. If that's the way you do things, then I'd rather have nothing. Now, if you'll excuse me, I have work to do."

Janty, sensing that he had been outplayed, grunted and disappeared behind a large painted canvas. Wilma shook her head. "In my experience," she explained to Pickle, "when boys make a fuss, it's because they want attention. We must try to make him see sense."

Pickle snorted again. He understood nothing of the mystery of small boys and the workings of their spinning minds, but he did know one thing—Wilma always looked for the good in people. So, as much as he would quite like to bite Janty, he wouldn't. For her sake.

"Hey, you! You with the messy hair," said a voice to their left. It was Loranda Links, the contortionist. "Have you seen Malcolm? He's supposed to help me grease up."

Loranda looked extremely glamorous. Her hair was a golden swirl of intricate braids studded with flashing jewels, the makeup around her eyes was deep and smoky, and her lips were a vivid red. Wilma, taking her in, was most impressed with Loranda's costume. She was wearing a green scale-decorated leotard cut to look as if she were being squeezed by a python. It was all very racy.

"He went off to find a hat," Wilma said, pointing. "That way, stage up, down-over-there."

Loranda held out a large, slippery tub. "Then you'll have to help me. I'm on second after the Great Sylvester. Just rub some of this onto my back, would you? And smear it on good and thick. Or my legs don't slide down so well."

Wilma took the tub and scooped out a large handful. It was cold and slimy. "Do you know Cecily Lovely?" she asked as she rubbed the grease into Loranda's shoulder.

"Of course I do," said Loranda, bending to stare at her face in a mirror. "She's the show's big star. Or so she likes to think. If you ask me, she's past it. Not that Gorgeous seems to notice. He's like a lovesick puppy around her. Does everything she asks. She's not remotely interested, of course. Oh! There was no love lost between Cecily and Sabbatica! Cecily can pretend she's upset, but we all know the truth. She's glad Sabbatica's dead! She'd be even gladder if we were all dead! You know why? Because she'd be the only one left on the bill. And poisoned too! The woman's weapon of choice. Probably sprayed it onto her! She's always wafting around with that atomizer of hers. Or got Gorgeous to bump Sabbatica off! They're probably in it together. And have you seen the crow's-feet around her eyes? She says she's twenty-seven! Fifty-seven, more like! If you want my opinion, she's a terrible singer. Anyway. Thanks for helping with my back. Let's hope I break a leg! Where's Scraps? I gave her my slipper to mend . . . Scraps! SCRAPS!"

"Goodness," whispered Wilma as the contortionist wandered off to limber up. "Don't theatrical types like to gossip! I don't think this case is going to take much probing at all!" She looked down at her sticky hands and tutted. "Covered in grease, Pickle. I think there was a handkerchief on the props table. I can use that to get clean."

Wilma's mind was so whirring with all the information she'd received that she failed to notice a shadow unfold from behind a painted flat to her left and vanish back into the darkness. The only thing that alerted Wilma to someone's presence was a creaking sound. Pickle's ears cocked. Wilma turned around. "Hello?" she called out. "Janty, is that you? Is someone there?" But nobody replied. Instead, out burst Malcolm, arms full of knives, which he dropped onto the props table.

"Excuse me! Excuse me!" he panted. "Safety curtain's going up! Show starts in one minute! Got to polish Mr. Sylvester's knives! Now, where did I put that cloth? Ah-ha!"

"Oooh," said Wilma, realizing that the cloth she'd wiped her greasy hands on was now being used to polish knife handles. "I don't know if that's a good—"

"My knives, Malcolm!" boomed an impressive-looking man in a pair of baggy pantaloons. He was bare-chested, had immense upper arms and a face that looked as if it had been chiseled out of granite. It was the Great Sylvester. "Trixie!" he added, turning to his scantily clad assistant. "Get into position on the target board!"

"Oooh, wait!" said Wilma, but to no avail. The orchestra had struck up their overture, the curtains were opening, and the Great Sylvester was striding onto the stage. A polite applause rippled through the audience.

"Still not many in," sighed Malcolm, taking a

quick peep through the side curtain. "Oh well. Have a good show, everyone!"

"Ladies and gentlemen!" the Great Sylvester roared, banging his knives together. "Prepare to stare death in the face as I throw these razor-sharp knives at my glamorous assistant."

Wilma rushed to the wing and grabbed the corner of the curtain there. Those handles were covered in grease! Somehow she had to do something. But before she could raise any sort of alarm the Great Sylvester, one arm aloft and knife poised, suddenly grabbed at his throat with his free hand and slumped to the floor. As he fell, the raised knife in his other hand slipped from his fingers and with the force of his fall, propelled itself through the air. There was a blood-curdling, devastating scream.

"Oh no, Pickle," said Wilma, hand reaching for her mouth. "I think I've just mucked things up spectacularly."

Oops.

Wilma could hardly bear to look. She'd only been enrolled as an official apprentice for a day and here she was, partly responsible for the instant demise of a woman in a sequined blouse, which she was pretty sure meant she had definitely broken Golden Rule number five! How was she going to explain this to Mr. Goodman? How would she ever forgive herself?

The detective and Inspector Lemone had come running down to the wings as soon as they'd heard Trixie's scream. When they got there, Wilma was still clutching the curtain, her face buried deep within it. Pickle, equally traumatized, was lying on the floor with his paws over his eyes.

"Oh no, Goodman," said the Inspector as he stared out on to the stage. "Looks like we've had another one."

"Wilma," said Theodore, pulling her face out of the curtain. "Did you see something? What happened?"

Wilma's wobbling chin was pressed against her chest. She couldn't look up at her hero. "I'm very sorry, Mr. Goodman. But I think I've caused a murder. The thing was, my hands were greasy. And I wiped them and then the cloth got used on the knives and then they were greasy and . . ." Very slowly, she unpinned her precious apprentice detective badge and held it up. "I expect you'll want this back."

"I'm fine, really," said Trixie, clutching her forehead as she was led past them by Malcolm Poppledore. "The knife only went through my sleeve."

Wilma whipped up her head. Trixie was alive! "Oh!" she cried with relief. "You're not dead!"

Inspector Lemone frowned. "I am going to put

my hand up and say that at this juncture I have absolutely no idea what anyone is talking about."

"I'm not sure that I have either," confessed Theodore as he patted Wilma reassuringly on the shoulder. "But one thing I do know—we have another body on our hands." And with that he strode onto the stage and bent down over the knife thrower's prone form.

The anxiety in the auditorium was palpable, a mixture of excitement and worry. "That sign was right!" someone called down from the Upper Dress Circle. "It is a stage of death!" Mutters and mumbles broke out.

"Please remain calm," Theodore pronounced, holding up a hand. "We will get to the bottom of this as soon as we can!"

"Not soon enough for the Great Sylvester!" shouted a young boy's voice. "Maybe someone else should be put in charge!"

The audience grumbled ambiguously.

"Pipe down!" shouted a thin, reedy-looking man who had stood up in the stalls. "Mr. Goodman is Cooper's most serious and famous detective!"

"Hear, hear!" yelled someone else.

"That he may be," came the boy's voice again from the shadows, "but there's still a second body on the stage!"

The audience murmured once more.

Wilma, standing in the wings, was aghast. "Why are they turning on Mr. Goodman?" she asked, looking up at the Inspector. "He's done nothing wrong."

"People need someone to blame, I'm afraid," explained Inspector Lemone. "Don't worry. Goodman won't let it bother him."

And, as the great detective returned to his companions with a worried frown, up high toward the back of the theatre, Barbu D'Anvers put a hand on Janty's shoulder. "Well done," he whispered with a small, evil laugh. "And so the game's afoot. Continue to rattle the girl. We'll have Theodore ruined in no time. And another death. Today's shaping up nicely. Very nicely indeed."

"Inspector," began Theodore with purpose, "I shall need statements from everyone at the theatre. With a second body, we must accelerate our investigations immediately. We are clearly not now looking at an accidental poisoning. Not only that, but whoever is behind this clearly has more than just a personal dislike for Sabbatica the mind reader."

"Mr. Goodman!" piped Wilma, running to keep up with him. "I was talking to Loranda Links, the lady dressed like a snake's dinner, and she thinks that Cecily Lovely hated Sabbatica and that she'd quite like to be the only person onstage."

"Then we shall start with her," said Theodore. "To Cecily Lovely's dressing room!"

Having established that the same stinking, yellowish foam was in the Great Sylvester's throat, pandemonium had broken out backstage and, as Wilma trotted behind Theodore and the Inspector, she couldn't help but notice the looks of panic on people's faces. Mrs. Wanderlip was standing with Claiborne Wordette, the bird impersonator, who was so sad, she was hooting like an owl while being comforted by a ventriloquist dummy, who, Wilma had to assume, was Eric Ohio. And Countess Honey Piccio was so distressed by the turn of events she was absentmindedly tearing paper into the shape of a host of Grim Reapers. Everyone, it would seem, was in pieces.

As they rushed toward Cecily's dressing room, an arm came out and stopped Theodore in his tracks. It was Mrs. Grumbletubs, the laundry mistress, with her son, Geoffrey. "You will find who did it, won't you?" she asked, her face filled with anxiety. "I don't care about myself. But it's my son. He's so young. I don't want anything to happen to him."

Wilma looked at Geoffrey and smiled. He didn't smile back. He was too busy screwing his face up into a tight ball of embarrassment. "Please don't, Mother," he whined. "I'm old enough to look after myself!"

Theodore placed a reassuring hand on Mrs. Grumbletubs's shoulder. "I can promise you that I will get to the bottom of this as soon as is possible. But for now remain vigilant. You too, young man. Nobody is too grown up to take a little extra care."

Geoffrey mustered something approaching a smile, but he was a teenager, so it might have been a trapped burp. When it comes to grumpy boys, it's sometimes very hard to tell.

"I cannot cope!" they could hear Cecily screaming as they approached her dressing room. "And you do nothing! You're hopeless! Get out! Get OUT!"

Gorgeous Muldoon, the comic compère, appeared suddenly in the doorway. "But, Cecily . . ." he was pleading.

"Get OUT!" At which Gorgeous ducked and a large man's shoe flew over his head and landed at Theodore's feet.

The detective bent down to pick it up. "An artistic difference?" he asked with a twitch of his mustache. Gorgeous scowled, put the tossed shoe on his foot, and limped off up the corridor muttering.

Wilma watched him go. "I wonder what's wrong with him?" she wondered out loud. "He's walking awfully strangely."

Cecily was slumped over her dressing table.

She was wearing a gown that was a mass of frills and a hat that anyone in their right mind would call ridiculous. It looked like a three-tiered wedding cake topped with figurines of a pair of pigs dancing.

Inspector Lemone was so startled by it that he had to wipe his eyes and look again. No. They were definitely dancing pigs.

Scraps, Wilma noticed, was standing next to an incredibly ornate silk screen, on top of which were draped various items of clothing. She had her head hung low and looked terribly nervous. Pots of preparations adorned the dressing table and next to them were a small pestle and mortar and a crushed pile of rosemary.

"Miss Lovely," said Theodore, announcing their entry. "You will be aware that there has been another unfortunate incident. I wonder if I could trouble you with a few questions?"

Something under the heap of frills shuddered. Then, suddenly, like a melodramatic jack-in-the-box, Cecily's head sprang upward only to disappear again as she flung herself backward and let out a wail that was previously thought solely achievable by severely injured cows. "WHHHHHHYYYYYYYYYY?" she yowled. "WHHHHHHYYYYYYYYYY is this happening to me? To MEEEEEEEEEEE??!!" Everyone looked at one another. They didn't quite know what to do. Pickle, who always preferred to err on the side of caution, found a hat box and hid behind it.

"She's hysterical," whispered Inspector Lemone, fingering his collar. "I have no idea how to deal with this. None whatsoever."

"Hysterical? Of course!" said Wilma, holding a finger aloft. "Leave this to me." She stepped forward and, much to Miss Lovely's surprise, took her by the shoulders, shook her, shouted, "You are hysterical! Calm down!" and then, with one fulsome swipe, slapped her firmly across the cheek.

The diva gasped and clutched her face while staring at Wilma in openmouthed wonder. "Three S's, shake, shout, slap!" said Wilma with a nod. "Works every time."

Theodore, shooting Wilma a small but penetrating glance, cleared his throat. "Please excuse my apprentice, Miss Lovely. I'm sure she didn't mean to hit you."

"Well, I did," Wilma chipped in proudly. "It's an Academy thing where——"

"Never mind that now, thank you," interrupted Theodore before Wilma got herself into even deeper waters.

The actress, still glaring at Wilma, released her hand from her cheek. "Scraps," she whimpered, holding out a beckoning hand. "My handkerchief, if you please. And anoint it with that lavender water you made. I am feeling most weak."

"Yes, Miss Lovely," answered the raggedy hand-maiden with a small curtsy.

As Scraps turned to prepare the potion, Wilma caught her eye and if she wasn't mistaken she felt sure that she spotted the tiny beginnings of a smile in her direction.

Cecily lifted her other hand to her forehead and positioned herself in front of a particularly flattering light. "The thing is, Mr. Goodman," she whispered, eyes closed, "how can I perform if I no longer feel safe? This awful, sordid business is threatening the very fabric of my existence and, by association, Cooper itself."

"That's a bit of an exaggeration, surely?" muttered Wilma, crossing her arms.

Inspector Lemone looked down at her and put his finger to his lips.

"And what is more," Cecily continued, opening her eyes and staring wildly upward, "you have it wrong! I don't believe it is a poison! I think we are at the mercy of a terrible infection! A plague is upon this house! Do not tell me it's impossible!"

"Well," began Theodore, shifting on his feet, "I—"

"No, I'm not finished yet. Your cue will come shortly," snapped Cecily. "Do not tell me that a deadly virus cannot be crawling through every pipe and corridor of this theatre! And what can stop that, Mr. Goodman? A pair of handcuffs? I think not!" She slammed her fist down on her dressing table and collapsed her head into her chest. Nobody spoke. "Now it's your cue," she added, after a brief silence.

"Well," Theodore began again, "I suppose that, yes, we could be dealing with a virus. We haven't had results back from Penbert at the lab yet, so, although I suspect it's not, I cannot at this point rule it out."

"I have my answer!" Cecily yelled, standing up and knocking Scraps, who was trying to hand her the now lavender-laden handkerchief, over in the process. "Then there is only one solution! The theatre must be closed! The show"—Cecily stopped for dramatic effect and then continued—"the show must NOT go on!"

And with that she bundled everyone out of her way and stormed off up the corridor. Theodore, Inspector Lemone, Wilma, and Pickle were stunned. "Hang on," said Wilma, scratching her head. "We didn't get to ask her one single question . . . How did she manage that?"

"Well," answered Lemone with a small shrug, "she is a very good actress."

An actress with a notion in her noggin can be as dangerous as an untethered bear, and as Cecily tore through the corridors of the Valiant Vaudeville Theatre to find Baron von Worms, everyone knew to stand well back. Geoffrey Grumbletubs, who was so used to being at the receiving end of one of Cecily Lovely's hurricane tantrums that he had donned a tin helmet, grabbed his beloved potted plants and crammed himself and them into a small tea crate.

"Stop what you are doing!" she was crying as she swept along at speed. "A pestilence has descended! We may all be about to die! Or even worse . . ." she added, slumping suddenly against a wall at the very thought, "we may have to give up being famous! Oh, help me, Scraps! Help me!"

Baron von Worms, who, thanks to Barbu, no longer had an office, had tried to claw back some dignity by setting up shop in a small corridor behind the props room toward the back of the theatre. He had made himself a desk out of two cardboard boxes and an old scenery window. As he sat on an upturned hatbox, wondering what to do with himself, Cecily, closely followed by a tripping Scraps, descended.

"Baron!" she panted, hands on hips. "The theatre must be closed this instant! How I am expected to hit my high notes under these conditions I do not know! The theatre is in the grips of a deadly outbreak! Who is next? A plague strikes at will without regard for beauty or talent! First Sabbatica, now Sylvester! I am in the gravest danger, Baron! Me! Cecily Lovely! Struck down in the prime of her youth!"

Loranda Links, who was standing in the small crowd that had gathered, coughed. "Youth?" she choked out.

"B-but I thought Mr. Goodman told us it was a p-poison?" stuttered the Baron.

"It's highly likely that it *is* a poison, yes," said Theodore, pushing his way through the gathering. "But Miss Lovely pointed out that it might be a virus and I suppose, until we have definitive results from the lab, that it remains a possibility."

"The theatre MUST be closed!" screamed Cecily, throwing her arms into the air. "I might DIE! Do you understand?" And with that she slumped onto Scraps and wailed uncontrollably.

Wilma peeped out from behind Inspector Lemone. "Has she gone hysterical again?" she asked. "Shall I——?"

"Do nothing, thank you, Wilma," Theodore shot back in a flash. "I have to say, although Miss Lovely's assessment is far from likely, it might, in the circumstances, be wise to at least consider closing the theatre."

"CLOSE the theatre?" snapped Barbu, sweeping through, Tully and Janty fast behind him. "We shall do nothing of the sort. I need to protect my investment. I have put money into this theatre and I expect to make a sizeable return! As long as I am in charge of the Valiant Vaudeville Theatre it will NEVER go dark. In fact, I'm glad everyone is here. Seeing as we've had another death, I am increasing the daily shows from two to four as of Monday."

A gasp rang out among the theatre's performers.

"You can't do that!" snapped Gorgeous Muldoon. "It goes against every rule in the book!"

"Rules?" scoffed Barbu, knitting his brow. "*I* make the rules! I now control this theatre and I can do what I want. You will all be working twice as hard for half the money. There. Do you understand THAT?"

"This is an outrage!" cried out little Eric Ohio, his puppet head spinning a full 360 degrees.

"He's livid," whispered Mrs. Wanderlip. "I haven't seen him like this since someone tried to rub his legs together and start a fire."

Cecily, who was appalled to the point of collapse, glared at Barbu. "I don't know who you think you are," she began, mustering herself to her full height, "but if you think I'm going on FOUR times a day for HALF the money, you must be out of your tiny mind."

"Oooh," mumbled Tully, throwing Janty an anxious look, sensing there might be trouble.

"Sorry?" answered Barbu, cocking his head to one side. "Did you just call my mind 'tiny'?"

"Yes!" snapped Cecily, her eyes enraged. "Tiny! Tiny! Tiny! I shall not go on! I refuse to go on! And without me you have no show!"

Barbu looked up at her and scowled. A terrible, tense silence filled the air. Suddenly he twirled his cane in a jolly fashion and leaned back with a smirk. "Fine," he said with a shrug. "Don't go on. I shall just send on your *understudy*."

The silence continued as all eyes were fixed on the enraged diva. Cecily, who thought she had won her battle, blinked and swallowed deeply. "My . . . understudy?" she muttered with a shake of her head.

"Yes." Barbu smiled. "If you don't want to go on—fine. I shall send someone else on in your place. Someone *younger*. And *more attractive*."

Cecily blinked again and then, without warning, fainted very dramatically back into the group of performers behind her.

"She'll go on, Mr. D'Anvers," said Scraps, running forward as everyone tried to get Cecily to her feet. "Don't worry. She's a trooper."

"And that goes for the lot of you," Barbu barked, raising his cane and pointing. "You are all replaceable! Tully! Janty! Back to the office! We have plans to make!"

And with that he swept away, leaving a scene of chaos behind him.

Janty caught Wilma's eye and smirked. "Didn't they tell you at the Institute that it's rude to stare? Oh, but hang on—staring is all you can do." And before Wilma could respond he was gone, chasing after his evil master.

Wilma looked down at her beagle, who was trying to hide behind her legs. "Don't worry," she said, giving his ears a little rub. "I'll be doing more than staring. All the same, this is a strange case, Pickle, and no mistake."

To which the poor hound could only make a series of uncontrollable smells.

"I've drawn a picture of a virus for the Clue
Board, Mr. Goodman," said Wilma, flapping
a piece of paper in front of him. "I wasn't sure
what one looked like so I made it half crocodile,
half camel. That's the most dangerous thing I can
imagine. Shall I pin it up?"

Theodore stopped reading that morning's
Sunday Early Worm paper and examined the picture. "I think a piece of paper with the word
'virus' written on it will be sufficient, Wilma,"
he replied after a short period of serious contemplation. "After all, it's only eight a.m.—we're

still waiting for the results from Penbert. And my detective's hunch tells me we're probably dealing with a poisoner rather than a humped animal with crocodile jaws. And not only that, remember, but a poisoner who has a grudge against more than one person."

Wilma felt a little crestfallen, but tried hard not to show it. She was an apprentice detective now and had to get used to small disappointments. She folded her picture up and tucked it back into her pinafore pocket. Mr. Goodman put down his Sunday paper and reached for the ink pen in his waistcoat pocket. The evening show at the Valiant the night before had passed without incident, allowing the detective some valuable deducting time. Getting out his detective's notebook, he began to make notes. Wilma knew that when her mentor was contemplating and deducting she was expected to remain quiet, something she found very difficult to do.

She wandered over to the Clue Board, put a finger to her lip, like she'd seen Mr. Goodman doing when he was contemplating, and tried to fill the time with a small ponder. "The thing is, Mr. Goodman," she began, spinning around, "Cecily Lovely went to a lot of trouble not to get questioned."

"She did, yes," replied Theodore, still note-making.

Wilma chewed her bottom lip. "Did I tell you about when the Great Sylvester died, Mr. Goodman? You know, for clues and things?"

"Yes, you did, Wilma," replied the detective without looking up. "Four times as I recall."

"And everything that Loranda Links told me?" she added.

"Yes, that recollection lasted a full twenty-five minutes," mumbled Theodore, tapping his notebook with his pen.

"Hmm." Wilma nodded, blinking hard. "And did I tell you about the creaking noise when I was at the props table? I think someone was listening when I was talking to Loranda."

Theodore looked up. "Creaking?" he asked. "What sort of creaking? It's an old theatre. It could just have been the floorboards."

"No," said Wilma with a shake of her head. "It wasn't a woody sort of creak. It was something else. But I can't quite think what."

Theodore pondered and made a note. Wilma beamed. It was important to show Mr. Goodman that she was taking her apprenticeship seriously.

"You will not believe what I've found out!" announced Inspector Lemone, bursting in through the study door. He was holding an envelope in his hand and waving it. "I've got the insurance documents for the Valiant. They were sent to the police station this morning! Have a look at that, Goodman!" he cried, throwing it down on the detective's desk. Theodore took the envelope and opened it. "Hello, Wilma," added the Inspector, giving her head a quick pat. "Oh," he said, looking down at his suddenly sticky hand. "I think you've got some jam in your hair. Or something."

"Probably," replied Wilma, climbing up onto the chair in front of Theodore's desk so she could get a better look. "What does it say, Mr. Goodman?"

"It's an insurance policy, Wilma," explained

Theodore, standing up to read it. "That's a document that lets people who have things make sure that if those things are damaged or lost, then they can be financially compensated. And this tells me that there is a large insurance payout due to the Baron in the event of unnatural deaths. Interesting."

Wilma, chin cupped in her hands on Theodore's desk, tried to look as serious as she could. "I see." She nodded. "So, because there have been two unnatural deaths, the Baron will get constipated?"

Theodore cleared his throat and looked out of his study window for a moment. "Compensated, Wilma," he replied eventually. "Not constipated. That's something very . . . different."

"Here's the mail from yesterday, Mr. Goodman," said Mrs. Speckle, waddling in with her knitted tray. "You didn't have time to look at it last night."

Inspector Lemone, who was always romantically startled whenever he was in Mrs. Speckle's presence, automatically reached for his hair and flattened it.

Mrs. Speckle stopped and squinted at him. "You have strawberry jam smeared across your forehead, Inspector," she said with an unimpressed glare.

Inspector Lemone grimaced. Oh well. At least she'd looked at him. It was a start.

Theodore was still thinking about the insurance policy as he reached for the two letters on Mrs. Speckle's tray. "We shall have to talk to the Baron about this," he pondered. "And bump him up to Prime Suspect on the Clue Board, please, Wilma. And pin the policy on the Motives section. Oh," he added, waving one of the envelopes in the air. "This one is addressed to you, Wilma. Academy crest too."

Wilma scampered back to take it. Pickle, who had been snoozing in front of the study fire, opened one eye and made ready. If it was important, then he might consider getting up. If it wasn't, then he would stay where he was. There was absolutely no point in giving up the toastiest spot in Clarissa Cottage unless he really had to. Watch and learn, children. Watch. And learn.

Wilma, grinning with expectation, opened the letter and read it.

Dear Wilma Tenderfoot,

I hope your Missing Relative investigation is going well. If it's not, here is a tip.

Work backward. That's it.

Best wishes,
Kite Lambard

P.S. I'm also enclosing a few tags with your name on them in case you want to stitch them into the backs of things.

Wilma frowned. "Work backward?" she muttered, turning the letter over to see if there was anything else on the back. Nothing. Well, this wasn't much to go on. Being a pupil at the Academy of Detection and Espionage was clearly going to be tricky and mysterious. But perhaps that was the point. She'd have to think about it later. She had too much to do as it was. As much as she would like to devote her time to her own investigations, it was far more important to follow orders and help with the case at the Valiant. Personal matters would have to wait. Still, the tags were lovely. She poured them into her pinafore pocket.

"Inspector," Theodore said suddenly in a dark, troubled tone. "I think you should see this."

Inspector Lemone took the letter held out to him. "Well, I never," he said, scanning it quickly. "Think it's the killer?"

"What is it?" asked Wilma, running over. Pickle, who had happily gone back to snoozing, opened one eye again and cocked an ear. Wilma peered across Inspector Lemone's arm. The letter that Theodore had been sent was a collage of cut-out letters.

WHICH ACTORS WILL BE CORPSING NEXT WEEK?

"It's made of cut-up paper," Wilma noted. "Oooh . . . There's that lady at the theatre who tears bits of paper . . ."

"Countess Honey Piccio," said Theodore. "Hmmm. It seems we suddenly have a rush of clues and suspects. Put this in an evidence bag and pin it to the Clue Board, please, Wilma." Theodore clasped his hands behind his back. "Corpsing has a double meaning. In theatrical terms, it means to laugh when you're not supposed to. But given recent events, it clearly has a more sinister overtone."

"Very sinister indeed, I'd say," said Inspector Lemone, looking concerned. "Do you think there's going to be another murder next week?"

"Hard to say," answered Theodore, pacing. "Although I'm afraid we must assume that there will be. But why would the killer want to warn us? Surely every killer needs the element of surprise? It's almost as if the killer *wants* an audience. There's more to this than meets the eye, Inspector. Fetch the tandem! We're off to the Valiant!"

Pickle sighed and made a half-hearted attempt at a stretch. Things were taking a nasty turn. He was going to have to get up. And there he was, thinking if he snoozed through, he might miss all the horrible bits.

Yeah. Right.

As Wilma bounced along in the trailer on the back of Theodore's tandem, she sat, arms crossed and lips pursed, deep in thought and contemplation. They were on their way to the Valiant, as Theodore, given the morning's revelation, wanted to speak to Baron von Worms urgently. Wilma's thoughts, however, were on the letter she had received from her headmistress. The Clue Board she had made for the Case of the Missing Relative earlier that morning in her bedroom was alarmingly empty. In the middle there was a hand-drawn picture of herself, a piece of Mrs. Speckle's leftover Wellington wool stretching from that toward an old photograph of the Institute for Woeful Children and then to the luggage tag that had been left tied around her wrist when she was abandoned. Upon it were the words that had haunted Wilma ever since—*because they gone.*

"There's not much to go on, is there, Pickle?" she shouted to her beagle, whose ears were flapping in the wind. "Maybe if I try to think in a wonky way it might bubble up something useful . . . Ten years ago," Wilma began, thrusting a finger upward into the air, "I was left at the gates of the Institute for Woeful Children on a night so stormy the tree in the front yard was struck by lightning and split in two. I know that because whenever anyone asked about the tree Madam Skratch used to say it had happened on the night I'd arrived, and it was an omen that proved I was no good and probably rotten. She was wrong. I am neither. Nobody saw who left me at the gates, but, whoever it was, I don't think it was my parents or a relative. The luggage tag refers to 'They' and not 'We'! It was also written by someone who's not very good at grammar. Mr. Goodman always tells me to look out for that. The luggage tag should have read 'Because they HAVE gone' and then told us *where* they have gone." Wilma gripped the sides of the trailer as they bumped over a pothole. "But it did not. So I think the person who left me at the Institute won't be a really clever person like Mr. Goodman or Penbert. It will be . . ." Wilma stopped and then, with a quick adjustment of her goggles, delivered her big conclusion: "Someone else!"

Pickle gave a small huff of encouragement. One of a dog's basic duties is to show support at all times, even in the face of utter hopelessness.

Wilma reached for the notebook in her pinafore pocket and opened it to the page where she had previously made some scribbles. "What was that bit I found before in my Academy textbook? 'Relatives can be slippery and easily lost,'" she read out, over the wind. "'The first thing you need to establish is who the last person was to have contact with them.'" She stared up at the cloudless sky, deep in thought. "That's it, Pickle!" she announced, snapping her fingers. "Miss Lambard's letter! Work backward! We need to go *back* to my beginnings! And that means . . . we need to speak to the only person I know who might be able to tell me something . . . Madam Skratch. Prepare yourself, Pickle. We're going to have to go back to the Institute for Woeful Children!"

Pickle did his best not to look startled, but the thought of returning to that dark, forbidding place made him very nervous. So he made an involuntary smell. Just to register his feelings on the matter.

The Valiant was peculiarly quiet that morning, but then it was a Sunday, when there were no shows. Thankfully Barbu D'Anvers and his cronies were nowhere to be seen, leaving Theodore to conduct his investigations in a bit of peace.

"I can assure you I had nothing to do with it!" protested Baron von Worms as Inspector Lemone presented him with the potentially troublesome insurance policy.

"It's there in black and white!" pressed the Inspector, tapping the policy with his finger. "In the event of unnatural deaths, you stand to make a fortune! Now wiggle your way out of that one!"

Wilma was impressed. It was almost as if Inspector Lemone knew what he was doing and he *did* look really rather pleased with himself. He'd *never* solved a case without Goodman before, but there was always a first time and this was obviously it!

Theodore, who had let his friend take the lead, tapped some rosemary tobacco into his pipe and sat down on the tea crate in front of the Baron's makeshift desk. "How many people knew about this policy, Baron?" he asked gently.

"Nobody!" blustered the Baron, breaking out into an uncomfortable sweat. "Although the document was in my office. I suppose someone could have snuck in and read it, though I usually locked the door . . . But I didn't kill Sabbatica or Sylvester, Mr. Goodman! You have to believe me!"

"A pretty tale!" shouted the Inspector, rising to his part. "Nothing but flimflam and gobbledygook! I ought to clap you in irons this very instant!"

"That will do, Inspector," said Theodore calmly, raising his pipe to his mouth and lighting it.

"It's a standard clause in any theatrical insurance policy!" wailed the Baron, looking increasingly frantic.

"But you must concede that it looks very bad for you. Very bad indeed," reasoned Theodore, standing. "However, our inquiries are still ongoing. It's not impossible that someone is trying to use this against you. Obviously we shall have to see your bank records, Baron. It still really could be anyone."

"Well, I wish you'd said," mumbled the Inspector with a small pout. "Got myself all worked up. Thought I'd cracked it."

"Oh, I fear there's a long way to go before we crack this case, Inspector," replied Theodore, giving his friend an encouraging pat on the shoulder.

"There!" declared a voice from the corridor behind them. "You heard it from the man himself! He hasn't got the first clue what he's doing!"

Theodore frowned and peered into the dimly lit passageway. A group of people scribbling furiously on notepads were being led by Barbu D'Anvers, who was strolling toward the detective with an evil smirk on his face, Janty close behind. "Members of the Cooper press, Theodore," he announced with a grand sweep of his arm. "They've come for an update on the latest goings-on at the Stage of Death! I'm sure they'll pay particular note to the fact that you are getting nowhere with this case . . ."

Theodore's jaw set tight. "That's not what I said, Barbu, and you know it."

"Lah-dee-dah," trilled the tiny villain with a twirl of his cane. "Have you captured the perpetrator of these foul deeds? I think not. Ladies and gentlemen of the press, I stand before you, the Angel of the Valiant! And all my efforts to save it are being endlessly hampered by this man's incompetence!"

"Why, I . . ." spluttered Inspector Lemone, incensed to within an inch of his life.

Theodore reached for his overcoat. "These things take time."

"But what if there are further deaths in the interim?" pestered one of the journalists eagerly. "Will they be on your conscience, Mr. Goodman?"

"That'll do," butted in Inspector Lemone. "No questions during investigations! You know the rules! Now leave Mr. Goodman be and let him get on with his job!"

As the Inspector bundled Theodore away down the corridor, Janty turned to the press and added, "Running away. Theodore P. Goodman is *running* away. Make sure you all get that, won't you?"

Wilma and Pickle, who had yet to take off after their mentor, glared at the smirking boy before them. "Your boss is half the man that Mr. Goodman is!" Wilma snapped, arms crossed in anger. "In more ways than one!" she added with a withering head-to-toe glance toward Barbu. And before the villain could explode in response, she turned on her heel and ran after the Inspector and Mr. Goodman, with Pickle close behind.

"What's D'Anvers up to?" muttered the Inspector as Wilma and Pickle scampered toward them. "I don't like it, Goodman! Don't like it one bit!"

"Trying to muddy the waters, I expect," replied Theodore, who was consulting his notebook. "Diversionary tactics. It's standard criminal procedure. I wouldn't let it bother you. We've got far too much to do. Now then. Until we can establish how the victims were poisoned, the Baron must remain our chief suspect. But we also cannot rule out the fact that the real killer may be using a knowledge of that insurance policy to point a finger in his direction. The good news is that there are no shows today. Wilma, you can use the rest of the morning to start your Academy assignment. I heard you say you wanted to return to the Institute. Do so, but tread carefully. And I want you to meet me at the lab at two p.m. Inspector, you and I will return to Clarissa Cottage. I have a lot of contemplating to do."

Wilma was in no doubt about it. The contemplating to be done was *enormous*.

Cooper Island, as everyone knows, is divided into two parts. There's the affluent and well-to-do Farside and the lowly, trod-upon Lowside. The walk to the Lowside was a pleasant one. The Cooper poppy fields were in bloom, the pig poke was teeming with piglets, and because it was a Sunday morning people were out and about playing Skrittles, a throwing game where everyone tosses ten bowling pins toward one large ball. But as Wilma strolled through the depot at Measly Down, the village that was home to the border-control station, the relaxed air changed to one of bustle and confusion. Sunday was everybody's day off and all the Lowsiders who worked on the Farside were lining up to return home.

The Farside–Lowside border-control station was manned by a uniformed gentleman called Trevor. Wilma's experience of getting past Trevor had, in the past, been fraught with difficulties, but, with her apprentice detective badge pinned proudly to her pinafore, she was confident that her passage into the Lowside would be as easy as sneezing.

As Wilma and Pickle approached the border, the line was massive, but now that Wilma was on official business she'd be able to use the fast-track lane. Or so she thought. Wilma glanced up at the large round clock face that hung on a hook above the control booth. "Ten o'clock," she noted. "That gives us plenty of time to get to the Institute and then meet Mr. Goodman at the lab at two. In fact, Pickle, seeing as we're going on to the Lowside, we could go to Filthy Cove on the way to the Institute and see if we can find out more about the seaweed I saw in that bucket. I'm sure it's a proper clue! And then we'll go and see Madam Skratch! Perfect."

Pickle didn't respond. He had found a particularly stinky lump of something indefinable on the floor.

"Well, well," said Trevor, shoving his cap up his forehead when he saw Wilma approach the fast-track lane. "We meet again."

Wilma smiled. On her way to the border-control station she had decided on a brilliant tactic in order to navigate it better this time: She was going to be charming. "Hello." She beamed. "I'd like a day pass into the Lowside, thank you. In fact, I only need to be here for an hour or so. I hope you're well. I'm an apprentice detective now. Isn't it a lovely day? The poppies in Measly Down are wonderful. Have you lost weight? You look good. Younger. Not that you looked fat or old before. Is that a new hat? It really suits you. Not that your hair isn't lovely so it needs covering up . . ."

Trevor took off his cap and scratched his head.

"Oh," Wilma continued, gulping. "You haven't

got any hair . . . Well, it's still a very nice hat. So that'll be a day pass. For me. And my dog."

"Apprentice detective, eh?" growled Trevor, leaning over his desk and peering down at Wilma. "New position, is it?"

"Yes," answered Wilma, proudly pointing to her badge. "I've been enrolled at the Academy of Detection and Espionage, and Mr. Goodman has taken me on!"

A smug smile crept across Trevor's face. "Then you'll have to fill out all of these in quadruplicate," he said, reaching for a mass of forms. "This one's Change of Status. That one's Official Badge Recognition. The one under that is for the Apprenticeship Away-day Travel Card request. You'll need this one as well. That's the Increase in To-ing and Fro-ing Expectancy declaration. And, last but not least, you need to fill out this purple one as well."

"What's that one for?" asked Wilma, teetering under the mass of papers.

"It's not really for anything. We just like the color," replied Trevor, picking up a toothpick and sticking it between his front teeth.

Wilma was quietly seething. Still, there was nothing to be done. People in uniform with too much time on their hands are extremely fond of bureaucratic red tape. Filling out everything in quadruplicate was bad enough, but the Official Badge Recognition form required a brass rubbing of the badge in question, the Apprenticeship Away-day application needed a short essay on steam engines, and the To-ing and Fro-ing declaration had not only to be completed four times but also to be folded into the shape of a leaping frog.

"Well!" said Wilma an hour later, ink-covered legs splayed on the floor and surrounded by crumpled paper. "That's the best I can do!" Gathering up all of the completed forms, she approached the booth and handed them over to Trevor.

"This," said Trevor, holding up the folded To-ing and Fro-ing declaration, "looks more like a jumping toad than a leaping frog. I'm not sure it's going to be acceptable."

Wilma said nothing. She wanted to say quite a

few things at that precise moment, but Mr. Good-man always reminded her that proper detectives save what they're thinking till last. Especially when it might be a bit rude.

"We'll have to wait for an official adjudication," Trevor added, having a quick spin on his chair. "I can't let you in until we've had a ruling. My hands . . . are tied." He gave a half-hearted shrug in Wilma's direction. Wilma rolled her eyes. This was taking FOREVER. Just then, a fist holding a piece of paper shot out from a hole in the border wall. It was from the Grand Council of Border Controls.

All papers in order. Even if the folded bits were a bit terrible and toady. Access granted.

Love,
Kevin and Malcolm and Susan and Ian
(Official Border-Control Peepers)

A look of disappointment flitted across Trevor's face. "Oh," he said with a glum pout. "Then I suppose you can go through."

At last!

"Thank you very much, Trevor," said Wilma, and with a small but triumphant swish of her wayward hair she strode off into the Lowside, Pickle twitching his tail not far behind her.

Filthy Cove was on the easternmost tip of Cooper Island, just past the disused train tracks at Uppity Downs. Following a series of craggy footfalls, Wilma and Pickle were able to clamber their way down to a small, contained shoreline strewn with all manner of flotsam. There was a half-buried masthead, washed up after a wreck, the skeletal carcass of a long-dead whale, and a heap of unopened bottles, all of which had unread messages inside. Wilma kicked off her sneakers and trudged through the thick sand toward a series of rock pools. "According to the book *Shoreside Flora and Fauna* that I read in Mr. Goodman's study, the seaweed I found in the Baron's office is called Ascopopis Nodolum. It's called that because it has egg-shaped air bladders. That you can pop. Like this," explained Wilma, holding up the piece of seaweed from her pocket and popping one of the dried sacs between her fingers.

"Filthy Cove is the only place on the island where it can be found. Look. Here it is," she said, crouching down to reach the rock pool at her feet. "Ascopopis Nodolum. Pooh! It stinks!" She slipped a long, slimy length into her pocket.

Pickle bent closer to have a deep sniff, but as he did so a large crab, taking exception to being bothered, clamped one of its claws firmly onto the end of the poor beagle's nose. With a yelp, Pickle leaped into the air, lost his footing on the slippery rocks, and promptly fell headfirst into the freezing rock pool.

"Pickle!" chastised Wilma, yanking him out by the collar. "We haven't got time for fooling around."

Suddenly, Wilma sensed a figure darting to her right. She spun around, but before she could get a clear view of who it was a large wave crashed against a rock, sending a blanket of spray upward. Spluttering and rubbing the stinging seawater out of her eyes, Wilma strained to see who had been on the beach, but the figure appeared to have vanished.

"Drat!" she yelled, wringing seawater out from her pinafore. "Gone! And we saw nothing!" she wailed, thumping her fist downward in frustration. "Who could it have been? One thing's for sure: Whoever it was, was in a rush to get out of here without being seen and, if I remember rightly from the chapter in my textbook about Fleeing Suspects, that tells me they were up to no good!"

Wilma looked around her. "There must be something," she mumbled. "People who dash off generally don't have time to cover their tracks."

Pickle, who despite shaking himself down was still sopping wet, dripped forward and began pawing at the sand behind an old discarded lobster pot.

Wilma jumped over a rock to see what he had found. "Footprints!" She beamed. "We can see them in the wet sand. Well done, Pickle. They go back there to that rock pool." She scampered over to take a look. "There's a jam jar. And it's filled with Ascopopis Nodolum seaweed! I knew it meant something! And . . . oh my goodness . . . it can't be . . ." Wilma gently lifted up the jam jar by the metal hoop it was attached to. Hanging off the handle, by a tiny leather attachment, was one small, wooden finger.

"Well, there's only one person with a wooden finger at the Valiant, isn't there, Pickle? Mr. Goodman was right," she whispered as she placed the tiny but amazing clue into a Clue Bag. "This case is *filled* with suspects . . ."

The Institute for Woeful Children was as dark and foreboding as Wilma remembered it: the all-too-familiar turrets like upturned claws, the huge front gates lined with a row of cawing iron crows as terrifying as they had ever been, but when Wilma walked through them and saw the tree in the front yard, famously split in two on the stormy night of her arrival at the Institute, her resolve strengthened. She had come to do a job. And do it she would.

"Wilma Tenderfoot!" snarled Madam Skratch as she answered the miserable dull toll of the front doorbell. "Please don't tell me you're back."

Madam Skratch was what an independent panel of experts would call "revolting." She looked like a vulture and gave off an odor of over-boiled Brussels sprouts. Being the matron of the Institute for Woeful Children, her dealings with Wilma had, for ten years, been thorny and troublesome. So, as she stared down her considerable nose at the small child in front of her, she made a face that might lead some to believe that something dead had crawled up her nostrils.

"Actually," said Wilma, putting her thumb behind her apprentice detective badge and lifting it up for the matron to see, "I'm here on official detective-type business in my capacity as apprentice detective in the employ of Mr. Goodman— he's a detective—and as an enrolled student at the Academy of Detection and Espionage and under the tutelage of Headmistress Kite—"

"Yes, yes!" snapped Madam Skratch, curling her lip. "That'll do. I'm not in the least bit interested. What do you want? And make it snappy. I have children to beat."

Wilma cleared her throat. It was quite daunting to be standing in front of her old matron, but right now Madam Skratch was the only tangible link to her past and, frightened or not, Wilma knew she was going to have to bite the bullet and work backward. "I've had a quick read of my Academy textbook," Wilma began with a gulp, pulling it out from her pinafore pocket, "and it's got a whole chapter on Inquiries and Questions." She held it up for Madam Skratch to look at.

The matron batted it away with her bony fist. "Blah, blah," she said. "Get to the point, Tenderfoot. I don't have all day."

"And I was wondering if you had anything else you could tell me about the night I was left here? And who left me? And why they left me? And where I came from? And how you know I've got a relative alive somewhere? And where they might be? And whether you think they've got themselves lost? And, if so, where they might have lost themselves? And——"

"Stop!" yelled Madam Skratch. "You're making my brain spin! You really are a thorn in my side, Tenderfoot! Still, the sooner I answer your questions, the less likely I am to ever see you again. All right! Let's get this over with. I don't know who left you. There was a basket and you were wrapped up in something. In fact, I've still got it somewhere. Every child that comes here gets a box. Everything from the basket was put into that. Along with the monthly letters that came. With the money. I don't know who sent them. And——before you ask——no, the money was not for you. It was for me. So you can't have it back. And, even if it was for you, you still can't have it back. Because I'm mean. And then another letter came. Just before you left here. From someone looking for you. But I only read half the letter because the second page was burned after Timothy Scraggens tripped and dropped it in the fire as he was delivering it to me. So I never knew who sent it nor did I have an address to reply to.

But they were definitely looking for you. There. That's it. That's all I know."

Wilma was agog. "A box? With stuff in it about me?" she asked, slightly trembling. "Can . . . can I have it?"

Madam Skratch stared down her considerable spiked nose at the ten-year-old in front of her. "Do you promise never to bother me again?" she asked, bending low and stabbing Wilma in the shoulder with her finger.

Wilma nodded, wide-eyed. "I promise."

"Then stand over there," Madam Skratch snarled, gesturing toward the courtyard. "I shall throw everything down from my study window. And then you will pick it up, leave the premises, and never return. Do you understand, Wilma Tenderfoot?"

"I do, Madam Skratch," replied Wilma, clutching the bottom of her pinafore. This was incredible. In her wildest dreams Wilma could not have imagined that she was about to receive a box filled with things that might help her find out where she had come from. Or where her relative might be. As the front door of the Institute slammed shut, she looked down at her faithful beagle. "Can you believe this, Pickle?" she asked wonderingly. "A whole box of clues!"

Even Pickle, who was rarely astonished, was so stunned that all he could do was stand with his tongue hanging out and look slightly cross-eyed. He shook his head. No. His eyes were still crossed. He hadn't been this surprised since he'd found out that jellyfish can't do the backstroke.

The window to Madam Skratch's study creaked open above them. "This is everything!" shouted down the matron, holding out a burlap sack. "I never want to clap eyes on you again, Wilma Tenderfoot!" And with that she hurled the sack from the window and then slammed it shut again with a bang.

Wilma ran to the dropped sack and, trembling, untied the rope around its top. Inside the bag there was a cardboard box stuffed with hundreds of letters. "Oh, Pickle," she whispered, dropping to her knees. "There are so many! And there's something else . . . down at the bottom . . . something white." Reaching in farther, Wilma pulled out a delicate, gauze-like material. "This must be what I was wrapped in," she pondered, holding it up to look at it. "It's a strange material. I wonder what it is."

But before she could do anything else the clock tower at the Institute began its melancholic chime.

"Oh no!" Wilma yelled, leaping to her feet. "It's one o'clock, Pickle! We need to get to the lab!" And grabbing the sack up and tossing it over her shoulder Wilma ran off through the Institute gates, Pickle fast behind her.

13

"**A**bsolute disgrace!" blustered Inspector Lemone, his cheeks a vivid red. "They don't know what they're talking about, Goodman!"

The Inspector had picked up the lunchtime edition of the *Early Worm,* Cooper's most popular paper, to read as he coasted along on the back of Theodore's tandem, only to discover the front page splashed with the headline FRIGHT NIGHT'S FLIGHT OF NO-GOOD GOODMAN!

"They're saying you ran away!" Inspector Lemone continued as the great detective pedaled hard in front of him. "Total rot and balderdash!"

Theodore, as well as being very serious and very great, was also very sensible, and as he looked over his shoulder at the offending headline he merely raised an eyebrow. "Don't give it a second thought, Inspector. Alarming events often lead to minor frenzies. We shall rise above it and continue with our inquiries. And I'd appreciate it if you did some pedaling, Lemone. It's quite a steep hill up to the lab."

"Sorry if I'm a bit late, Mr. Goodman!" Wilma called out, running up the path with Pickle toward the lab as Theodore and the Inspector were arriving. "Have I missed any deductions? You'll never believe what Madam Skratch gave me! Look! A whole box of clues. There's letters! And a strange piece of cloth! I'll be deducting this for weeks! Not only that, but I went to Filthy Cove and found the most amazing clue and . . ." Wilma was grinning, but noticing the Inspector's troubled expression she stopped. "Is something wrong?" she asked. "I'm not in trouble again, am I? Because I didn't mean to tip caramel into your rosemary-tobacco jar, Mr. Goodman. It just sort of happened."

"No, no, Wilma," reassured Theodore, dismounting and undoing the bicycle clips from the bottom of his trousers. "The Inspector is a bit cross about something he's read in the paper. Hmm . . . I'd wondered why my pipe was so sticky."

"*Bit* cross?" snarled Inspector Lemone, wiping the sweat from his forehead. "I should say! Ridiculous claims! Barbu D'Anvers is trying to smear Goodman's name! Look at that, Wilma!" he added, holding out the paper. "The nerve of it!"

Theodore stood tall and placed his thumbs in his waistcoat pockets. "As I said before, Inspector, we shall rise above it . . . Two people have been killed in startling circumstances. Until we find out who did it and why, the *Early Worm* needs to be cross with someone."

"Well, can't they be cross with someone horrible?" asked Wilma, a little puzzled. "Like Mr. D'Anvers? I don't understand why they should want to be cross with you. Although there was that time when I was at the Institute and all of

Madam Skratch's underwear went missing and I just happened to be on pant-folding duty and she was very cross with me. But I hadn't done it. I was just there."

"How . . . unexpected," said Inspector Lemone, who had almost calmed down.

"Yes," said Wilma, nodding, "it turned out a boy named Timothy Herrpip had taken all her underpants to make a gigantic catapult out of the elastic. Madam Skratch had VERY big underpants. But until she'd found out who'd done it, I got the blame. I suppose it's like that?"

"Sort of," said Theodore, clearing his throat a little. "Anyway, you said you'd found a clue at Filthy Cove . . ."

Wilma nodded and held out the bag with the wooden finger in it for Theodore to see. "I went down to the shore to collect some seaweed. Remember, I saw some in the Baron's office and thought it was an . . . anomaly . . ."

"Well done," said Theodore.

"And I looked up seaweeds in one of your reference books and found out that the only place I could find the same seaweed was in Filthy Cove. So I went there. And someone else was also there. Someone who ran off before I could get a good look at them. And whoever it was left a jam jar with some more seaweed in it and this was attached to it! It must have come off in the rush to get away."

Theodore took the finger and peered at it through his magnifying glass. "And who do you think this belongs to, Wilma?" he asked, one eye closed.

"Well, obviously Eric Ohio, Mrs. Wanderlip's dummy!" declared Wilma, panting with excitement. "It's the only answer!"

"Hmm. It would seem suspects are piling up," Theodore commented, twiddling his magnifying glass back into his waistcoat pocket with a flourish. "Onto the Clue Board with it, Wilma," he added, handing the finger back. "We shall have to contemplate this further. But first the lab! Penbert has some results at last."

Dr. Kooks's assistant had been waiting anxiously at the lab window. There were formalities to be performed whenever visitors arrived and she had had the guest badges lined up and ready to be handed out from the moment she had heard Theodore's tandem on the graveled path outside. The visitors' book was opened at the relevant page, the incident register was ready should a mishap occur, and her official white coat had been bleached and starched to within an inch of its life.

"Penbert!" bellowed Dr. Kooks, waltzing out into the reception area. "I've been working on a new song."

The preoccupied assistant turned to look at him. He was wearing a large spongy homemade hat that looked suspiciously like a big gray cauliflower, and a sheet that had a spine painted down its center.

Penbert blinked. "Where's your white coat, Dr. Kooks? Mr. Goodman is here. Have you forgotten?"

"Yes, yes," answered the eccentric scientist with a dismissive wave of his hand. "Never mind that. Guess what I am?"

Penbert didn't have time for this. Visitors were

imminent. There were badges to hand out, books to sign. "I don't know. Mr. Goodman is here. I'm a bit——"

"I'm a brain! Ah-ha!" declared the doctor, throwing his arms into the air. "It's for the song. Here goes." He cleared his throat and closed his eyes.

"If we didn't have a brain!
Then we'd surely be insane!
Or dribble like a big Great Dane!
We'd be a horse without a rein!
An empty head's a mental sprain!
If you haven't got a brain!
A brain! A brain! A brain, brain, brain!
A brain makes you urbane!
Gives you the fizz of pink champagne!
Complex sums you can explain!
And tells your bum to make methane!
That's a brain! A braaaaaaaaaain!"

Dr. Kooks, down on one knee, arms outstretched, opened one eye and looked up at his assistant. "Well, what do you think? I'm writing a musical about body parts. Think it might go down very well at the Valiant."

"Capital tune, Titus!" announced Theodore, standing in the doorway.

"I liked the bit about methane best," added Wilma. "Because it's true."

Pickle snorted in agreement. He loved everything to do with methane.

Penbert, slightly relieved that she wasn't going to have to pass judgment on her employer's woeful warbling, shoved her glasses firmly to the top of her nose and quickly signed everybody in, including Pickle. "Here are your visitor badges," she said, handing them all out. "You can return them when you're leaving. They're sort of new. So don't cover them in jam. Or use them as drinks coasters. Or poke holes in them and—"

"Penbert!" snapped Dr. Kooks, rolling his eyes. "That will do. Glad you liked the song, Goodman. I've been trying to write one about kidneys. But the only thing I can think of that rhymes with kidneys is Sidney's. And I don't know anyone named Sidney. Anyway! Results! You have come for results!"

"That we have, Titus!" replied Theodore with a smile. "Tell me everything you have discovered."

"Well," began Dr. Kooks, picking up a chemical beaker with some half-drunk tea in it. "We dissected the bodies. Although I say 'we,' actually Penbert did it. I was busy making this brainhat. Bit worried it looks like a misshapen potato, though. Might trim some off the back."

"It's definitely a poison, Mr. Goodman," said Penbert, stepping in and reaching for her clipboard. "I'm not quite sure of the source yet. It's an unusual organic compound."

"Organic?" asked Wilma. "Like a carrot?"

"In a way, yes," replied Theodore. "Penbert means the poison has come from a natural source. Like a plant."

"Or a carrot?" asked Wilma, pulling out her notebook.

"There are no known poisons that can be extracted from a carrot," stated Penbert with some force. "Sabbatica was not killed by a carrot. Let's nix that rumor from the start."

Realizing that Penbert looked quite agitated, Wilma decided she'd try a bit of encouraging. After all, everyone settles down with a kind word or two. "Not killed by a carrot!" Wilma declared, scribbling in her notebook. "At last we're making progress. Well done, Penbert. Please carry on."

Theodore shot a sideways glance at his young assistant and twitched his mustache. "So the poison has been extracted from a plant." He turned back to Penbert. "Do you know what plant?"

"Not yet, Mr. Goodman," said Penbert with a shake of her head. "The tricky thing is that the extract seems to be inert in its natural state."

"I have no idea what that means," said Wilma brightly.

"Don't worry," added Inspector Lemone, who had just found a forgotten muffin in his top pocket, "neither do I."

"It means that on its own it isn't dangerous. It needs something else to make it poisonous," Dr. Kooks explained.

"Fascinating," murmured Theodore, tapping his magnifying glass.

"Umm . . ." piped up Wilma, reaching for the long length of seaweed in her pocket. "It might be nothing, but there was seaweed in the Baron's office and so I thought I should go dotty with some *t*'s and get cross with an *i*."

Inspector Lemone frowned.

"Dot the *i*'s and cross the *t*'s, Wilma," corrected Theodore. "It means to make sure you have everything covered."

"Yes, I know. I read about it in my textbook," replied Wilma, handing the seaweed to Penbert. "So maybe you'd like to cross and dot that."

Penbert took the seaweed from Wilma using a large pair of tongs and placed it in a beaker. "Well, all right," she agreed reluctantly. "But just to be thorough."

"How does the poison work, please?" asked Wilma, who had gotten out her textbook and was looking at a page headed "Poisons and What Makes Them so Rotten."

"It attacks the lungs," explained Penbert, going

over to a diagram of a human body hanging above her desk, "creating a stinking foam that causes asphyxiation."

"Ass-fixy-what?" asked Wilma, screwing her face up.

"Asphyxiation," explained Penbert. "It means they can't breathe. In a sense, whatever we are dealing with is strangling the victims from the inside out."

"Absolutely ghastly," said Dr. Kooks with a shiver.

"And there's no evidence yet of how this poison is being administered?" asked Theodore, looking very serious.

"Unfortunately not, Goodman!" bellowed Dr. Kooks, tapping his sizeable stomach. "If we knew that, we'd have this case done and dusted!"

"Oh!" cried out Penbert suddenly. "No! Your beagle!"

Everyone turned and looked at Pickle. He had something in his mouth and the floor around him was covered in tiny bits of wood.

"My matchstick chicken!" moaned Penbert. "I've been making it for months."

"Oh, Pickle!" chided Wilma, rescuing the half-mangled model from her naughty dog's jaws. "How many times have I told you? Don't chew other people's matchstick chickens! Sorry, Penbert. Here. I think that's a beak. Or something."

"This will have to go in the incident register, of course," whispered Penbert, staring at the floor and biting her lip. "And I think I'll have my visitor badges back now, if you don't mind."

Strangled from the inside out? What a revolting turn of events.

"Not a dime," said Inspector Lemone the following day, shaking his head. "Went to the Cooper Bank first thing this morning. The Baron's account is empty."

"I see," answered Theodore as he tucked a copy of the post-lunch *Early Worm* under his armpit. "The fact he has no money in the bank may not be definitive. Money can be hidden in many places. And we're still awash with suspects. We need to find out how the poison is being administered. That's the key!"

"What about . . ." Wilma suggested as they

all paced into the Valiant to catch the end of the Monday matinee, "if the poison was hidden in Cecily Lovely's perfume? She could spray it onto anyone. And she does keep going on about being top of the bill and everything."

"It's not impossible," commented Theodore, taking a quick glance at his pocket watch.

"That seaweed," Wilma continued, on a roll. "Do you think it's important now, Mr. Goodman?"

"Possibly," replied the great detective, his brow furrowed with concentration. "But then, it's not the only plant we've seen at the theatre; the place is full of bunches of flowers."

"And potted plants, Mr. Goodman," added Wilma, wanting to be useful. "Geoffrey Grumble-tubs has loads."

Theodore looked pensive, but as the detective's team strode through the foyer, screams began to ring out from the auditorium. A double door ahead of them swung open and a woman, half collapsed, was being carried out. Wilma shot a quick look past her. The auditorium was surprisingly packed. "Two at once!" the woman wailed as she was dragged past. "The Stage of Death has struck again!"

"Looks like whoever sent that cut-up note means business, Goodman!" said Inspector Lemone with a troubled frown.

Theodore shot an urgent glance toward his companions and set his jaw with purpose. "Precisely! We must accelerate our efforts immediately. Inspector, you come with me to the stage. Wilma, I want you to ask everyone to meet me there. It's time I addressed the ensemble."

Two more people killed at the Valiant? Oh dear. Oh very, very dear.

"She's been passing out repeatedly since the killer struck again," explained Scraps, her face drawn with exhaustion. Cecily Lovely, her demanding mistress, was draped across a daybed, eyes wet with tears and a crumpled handkerchief clutched to her bosom. Scraps, Wilma noticed, looked terrible. She was covered in smudges, her gloves were gray and grubby, and she had no shoes on, just a pair of oversized socks. Wilma was about to offer her the remains of a corn crumble that she had in her pinafore pocket when Cecily began to come around again.

"Something . . ." the diva whispered, one hand shielding her eyes, "must be done. My nerves are in SHREDS!"

"Miss Lovely," began Scraps, wringing her gloved hands together, "Wilma's here because, if it's all right with you . . . your presence is required onstage. Mr. Goodman's got everyone there."

Cecily threw a shoe at Scraps, knocking her glasses to the floor. "No! Why should I do as he asks?" she screamed. "Have you not seen the papers? He hasn't the first clue what he's doing!"

Wilma bristled and tightened her lips. It made her feel a bit hot between the ears when anyone criticized Mr. Goodman, but, remembering what he'd said about "rising above it," she left the dressing room wordlessly, walking on her tiptoes.

"Technically speaking," Wilma said to Pickle, who was trotting at her heel, "she was hysterical.

But seeing as she was so rude about Mr. Good-man I decided not to cure her. She'll just have to bubble in her own froth! Poor Scraps. I'd hate to work for someone like that, wouldn't you?"

Pickle had to agree. There is *nothing* worse than a technically hysterical woman with an over-blown sense of her own capabilities.

The bodies of Claiborne Wordette, the bird impressionist, and Loranda Links, the contor-tionist, were being carried offstage. Sadly, their plan to go onstage together thinking there would be safety in numbers was woefully mistaken. The safety curtain had been brought down and as Wilma made her way toward Mr. Goodman and Inspector Lemone she could hear members of the audience calling out from the other side of it as they left the theatre. "Sack Goodman!" one man was yelling. "He's lost it!" shouted another. Clearly the stories in the *Early Worm* were begin-ning to have an effect.

"It's the same foam, Wilma," said Theodore, ignoring the protests. "It's now completely clear that, whoever this putrid poisoner is, he has got it in for everyone at this theatre. Have you asked everyone to gather on the stage?"

"I have, Mr. Goodman," answered Wilma. "But I don't think Cecily Lovely is coming. She's got herself into another tizzy-whizz."

Behind them, in the wings, the rest of the Valiant's cast and crew were gathering. Theodore's eyes narrowed as he gazed over at them, deep in thought. Wilma, remembering to look and learn, immediately tried to adopt a similar pose while also sneaking a good look at Mrs. Wanderlip and her dummy. She gasped. Tugging at her mentor's sleeve, she cupped a hand about her mouth and whispered, "Look at Eric Ohio's right hand, Mr. Goodman! There's a finger missing!"

"I know," whispered Theodore back. "Reveal nothing, Wilma. Remember your top tips."

Wilma nodded. All the same, this was a very exciting development. She nudged Pickle with her foot so he could take a look as well. But Pickle was distracted and staring at something on the floor. Wilma followed his eye line. There was a small gap in the stage boards a few inches in front of them and, as Wilma watched, a plume of dust puffed out of it. Wilma blinked. What could that have been? She stepped closer to take a better look. Another cloud of dust shot upward. Wilma blinked again. She knew that all stages have gaps underneath them but, in the circumstances, that puff of dust could be a clue! Perhaps there was a device that was administering the poison! Perhaps there was more than one person doing the poisoning! Over breakfast she had read the chapter in her textbook entitled "Criminals in Cahoots." They'd all been looking for one person. But what if there were two? She had to get under the stage and investigate!

Gesturing quietly to Pickle, Wilma crept off to a trapdoor in the wings that she had seen Geoffrey Grumbletubs using for storage and special entrances. Thinking detectively, Sabbatica must have used the other trapdoor, center stage, to come up through the floor on the night she died. Wilma, keen to show Mr. Goodman that she was advancing her detective techniques and making progress, tapped her notebook with her finger. "I know that I'm in a bit of doubt and the Golden Rules say I should stand quite still and do nothing, but top tip number three, Pickle," she whispered, "means I'm sometimes allowed to creep around after suspects. We can do that *and,* if we're lucky, catch someone doing some poison administering."

Lifting the brass circle of the trapdoor handle as gently and as silently as she could, Wilma lowered herself into the dusty blackened space. Pickle jumped in after her. Crouching to get her bearings, Wilma peered into the gloom. The under-stage area was packed with bits of broken scenery: there were window frames, a small tree lying on its side, and various painted panels, torn and dirty. Upright beams went from floor to stage at intervals, making the space seem maze-like and cramped. There were lots of places to hide, so Wilma knew she needed to be careful and cunning.

Being quite small (though very determined), Wilma was just able to walk upright without banging her head. Squeezing past a pyramid of greasepaint tubs, she began to creep toward the center of the stage. Suddenly, she heard a creak somewhere to her left. It was the same strange creak that she'd heard before the Great Sylvester died! She spun around quickly, Pickle barked, and from nowhere a sandbag swung into Wilma's face and she slumped to the floor.

Wilma didn't know how long she'd been unconscious, but it couldn't have been long, because above her she could still hear Theodore talking to the theatre cast. Pickle was struggling out from under a large burlap sack that had obviously been thrown over him. He emerged, panting, and began licking Wilma's nose.

"Oof," she spluttered, pushing him off her and raising a hand to her head. "Who did that? Where did they go, Pickle?"

The intrepid hound ran off a little toward the back of the below-stage area and then ran back again. It was clear that whoever had been there was now gone.

Pickle suddenly snorted and pointed his snout toward something trapped under the sandbag that had been thrown at Wilma.

Wilma crawled back toward it. "What is it, Pickle?" she mumbled as she struggled forward. "Looks like a bit of paper." Pickle yelped affirmatively. Lifting the sandbag with one hand, Wilma reached for the crumpled-up piece of paper with the other.

Must have been dropped in the scuffle, she thought, trying to focus. As she realized what she was holding, her eyes widened, all the pain in her head forgotten.

"Oh my goodness," she whispered, staring at what was in front of her. "This is the best clue EVER. Pickle! You're a genius. Mr. Goodman will be so pleased with us!"

And, as Wilma grabbed probably the best clue she had ever found and scampered back to the trapdoor, Pickle had to agree. He was a genius. Yes. He really was.

"I think she'll live," said Inspector Lemone, peering at Wilma's bump.

"You don't feel dizzy? Or disorientated?" worried Mr. Goodman.

"No. Don't mind me. I'll be fine." Wilma shot a quick look over her mentor's shoulder at the assembled cast and crew. "I heard that creak again, Mr. Goodman," she whispered. "But, better than that, look at what we found! It's an old playbill." Wilma held it out for her mentor to see. "It's two years old according to the date on the top. But here's the thing, Mr. Goodman. Everyone currently playing at the Valiant is on it. And look—everyone who's been killed has been *crossed off*!"

There was a gasp among the assembled players and staff.

"Blow me down!" muttered Inspector Lemone, peering over Theodore's shoulder. "So they have. You'll be a detective yet, Wilma!"

"It's like a shopping list, Mr. Goodman," Wilma continued, eyes wide with excitement. "Whoever is behind this is picking people off and deleting them from the list when they're done in and dead."

"So we're all doomed!" wailed Mrs. Wanderlip's puppet, Eric Ohio, his head spinning.

"This is a significant find, Wilma," said Theodore, taking the playbill from his apprentice. "Good work. But you must stop trying to pursue things on your own. Your safety is my responsibility, and I can't have you putting yourself at unnecessary risk."

Wilma nodded, but then she tugged at her mentor's sleeve and gestured at him to bend down closer. "There's more, Mr. Goodman," she whispered. "I think I might have deducted something vital. Did you notice anyone missing when I was under the stage? Because whoever wasn't here could have been down there with me, with that list . . ."

Theodore's mustache twitched. "I had thought of that, Wilma. But people were still gathering while you were gone. Well done, though; you're thinking like a detective."

Wilma turned pink with delight as Theodore addressed the cast and crew once more. "Ladies and gentlemen, somehow, someone is administering a poison with fatal consequences. I must therefore ask you to be at your most vigilant. Check that you are not eating anything unusual. Be alert to strange vapors, peculiar odors; in short, anything that seems out of the ordinary. And I think it would be best for all concerned if the theatre was closed immediately."

"Close the theatre?" said a voice behind them. "Put all these people out of work? Take away one of this island's finest institutions? Perhaps you'd all like us to stop enjoying sunshine and buttercups as well?"

Theodore turned and glared at Barbu, who had come to the stage with another pack of journalists behind him.

"I would much rather everyone was safe, D'Anvers," he replied sternly. "Not only that, but I cannot conduct a proper investigation while shows are ongoing."

"You? Conduct a proper investigation?" guffawed the undersized villain. "I hardly think so. A ten-year-old girl is managing to get better results than you!" he added, pointing at the playbill in Theodore's hand. Barbu turned to the scribbling reporters close on his heels. "Perhaps we should put Wilma Tenderfoot in charge of the case?"

"Make sure you spell her name right," scoffed Janty. "It's two *f*'s."

Wilma, horrified that somehow she might have gotten Theodore into deeper waters, stepped forward to protest. "I didn't mean to make Mr. Goodman look bad. I mean, he doesn't look bad anyway. I just saw a puff of something and went down to check it out. I didn't mean to do it."

"Stirring things up!" interrupted Inspector

Lemone, flushing red. "That's all you're trying to do, D'Anvers!"

"Did you hear that?" whined Barbu. "A veritable libel! When here I am, this theatre's only Angel, striving to get to the bottom of these ghastly, hideous, yet guaranteed to be quite regular, horrors."

"Very regular, Mr. Barbu," cut in Tully with a sniff.

"Probably be another one tomorrow," added Janty, picking a piece of dirt out from under a fingernail.

"This new development," said a small woman in glasses, holding up a pen. "Do you think it's the breakthrough you need to solve the case? Or should I address that question to your apprentice?"

A snigger rippled through the press pack.

Theodore, frowning, placed the playbill in his inside coat pocket. "We shall investigate everything thoroughly," he replied in a serious tone. "And we continue with our inquiries. Wilma, Inspector, given this press intrusion *and*

D'Anvers's refusal to halt the shows, I suggest we carry on our work back at Clarissa Cottage."

"Trotting off again," said Barbu with a theatrical shake of his head as the trio left. "Such a *shame*. He was great once, but I fear"—he paused for dramatic effect—"that Theodore P. Goodman's days are over. You can quote me directly on that. But to show that I am the Angel of this theatre, I shall let the cast have the rest of the day off. Make sure you put that in your paper. Maybe take a picture. I'll just stand on this box. You know, better angle. I'm not short."

The mood back at Clarissa Cottage was a sober one. Wilma, feeling terrible that she had inadvertently caused more trouble, was quietly penitent and instead of bouncing around Theodore's study as she normally did, sat herself in the corner, Pickle at her feet. Not even the arrival of Mrs. Speckle with a tray of peppermint tea and corn crumbles could lift her spirits. She had made Mr. Goodman look bad and she could barely forgive herself for it.

"Come along," rallied Theodore, seeing that his young apprentice was downcast. "We won't allow Barbu D'Anvers to make us feel gloomy. It's all part of his game-playing. Disrupting the case to protect his investment. He wants the murders to keep happening because it's good for business. Sadly, nothing excites people more than the prospect of ghoulish goings-on. The longer it takes us to solve the case, the more money he makes."

"The man has absolutely no morals!" blustered the Inspector, thumping his fist down on the arm of his chair.

"Now then, Wilma," added Theodore, "I've pinned the playbill you found to the Clue Board. Along with our other new findings: the information about the organic compound, thoughts on how the poison may be administered, the wooden finger, and your strange creaks, Wilma. So, let's see what you make of it."

"But . . ." began Wilma with a swallow, "am I allowed? I got you into so much trouble."

"We'll hear no more about it," urged the

detective, twiddling his magnifying glass. "We must expect a bit of rough and tumble from time to time. And, as professionals, we roll with the punches. Up you get. You found it, so let me have your thoughts."

Wilma knew perfectly well that Theodore could work things out by himself, but she was grateful she had a mentor who was so eager to cheer her up. Perhaps she could make amends with a brilliant deduction? So, scampering to the Clue Board and taking a handful of pins and a length of string, Wilma began to make a series of connections.

"Well," she began, sticking her first pin at the top of the playbill and drawing a piece of string down to a picture of Sabbatica. "Four actors are dead. All of them have been poisoned. By something planty . . . Geoffrey Grumbletubs likes plants . . . but there are flowers everywhere . . . and it still might be that seaweed."

Wilma added a bit more string down toward a picture of a bucket. "The strange thing is how we can't figure out how the poison is being given.

Or how it's being activated, but it must be done quite shortly before they go onstage because everyone seems fine until they start performing."

Wilma looked at Mr. Goodman to see how she was doing. So far, so good. Encouraged, she grabbed another length of string. "So, for some reason, this murderer hates actors. Which doesn't narrow down *anything,* but using only the power of my eyes and ears I have noticed that Gorgeous Muldoon walks funny, Eric Ohio is VERY temperamental, and Cecily Lovely is a pain in the neck. Oh! And the last thing," Wilma concluded, "is that all these deaths are making a lot of money. That's it. What do you think?"

The detective, who had gotten out his pipe and lit it while Wilma was so busy, stared at the mass of string and pins on the Clue Board. "Quite good," he said, giving out a small puff of smoke. "And your strings and pins have made the shape of a large duck. Intriguing."

Wilma stood back and looked at the Clue Board. So they had.

"Of course, you're missing something quite

fundamental," explained Theodore, walking over to the Clue Board and tapping the playbill with the end of his pipe. "There is something missing here. Look at the very bottom. It has been torn away. What do you think of that?"

Wilma peered closer. "Oh yes," she said, noticing the playbill's tattered bottom for the first time. "I wonder what was there. Looks like someone's trying to hide something."

"Exactly," replied Theodore. "This case is filled with torn bits of paper! Somehow we have to find out what was on the bottom of that playbill!"

"If only that dastardly D'Anvers wasn't making the investigation so danged difficult!" piped up Inspector Lemone. "He's making it practically impossible to proceed!"

"Perhaps we should do something wonky?" suggested Wilma with a renewed confidence following her successful deducting.

Theodore's eyes flashed upward. "Perhaps we should, Wilma," and then, with a determined bite on his pipe, he added, "And the sooner the better . . ."

"**B**usiness is BOOMING!" guffawed Barbu, staring up at the front of the Valiant. "If we carry on like this, I shall be rich beyond my wildest dreams! Canceling the rest of yesterday's shows has made me more popular than ever! They're lining up around the block to get in! Put that sign more to your left, Tully!"

"Yes, sir, Mr. Barbu," answered the stupid sidekick, wobbling a little on his ladder.

"I like your sign, Janty," added Barbu with a twirl of his cane. "It has the requisite oomph needed to pull in the people! *Stage Fright Nights!* It's almost brilliant!"

Janty smirked. "We're selling out, Mr. D'Anvers! Even with the extra shows you've put on. If I were you, I'd put on even more. Although we'd need more performers. But we can advertise for those. We could do shows on the hour every hour—we'd make a fortune!"

Barbu shot his charge a fierce stare. "*I'd* make a fortune. Not you. You just get to enjoy the glow of my excessive fabulousness. Hmmm . . ." Barbu's eyes narrowed as he stared upward, his lips pursed. "Something isn't quite right with the front of this theatre and I can't put my finger on it."

"Is it me, Mr. Barbu?" asked Tully, hanging off the Valiant Vaudeville sign, his ladder having fallen to the floor. "Because I'm not supposed to be here."

"No, you idiot!" snapped Barbu. "Although now you say that . . . I have it! It's the name of the theatre! The *Valiant* Vaudeville?"

"Named after Edward Valiant, Mr. D'Anvers," explained Janty. "He was a philanthropist and discovered a cure for blindness."

"He could cure the blind?" sneered Barbu.

"Why would anyone want to remember him? No! This theatre needs to be renamed. From now on it shall be known as the D'Anvers Vaudeville Theatre. See to it, Janty. Oh, and, while you're at it, let's change the word Vaudeville to Vau-DEVIL. I think that strikes the right note."

"And did you see this, Mr. D'Anvers?" added Janty, pulling a copy of that morning's *Early Worm* out from his back pocket. "Look at the headline. Thought you might like it."

Barbu flicked open the paper. "GOODMAN FINISHED? Oh. Well, that's perfect. With the money I'm making and Goodman out of favor, I shall have this island in my grip before we know it!" He grinned at Janty. "I think it's time for an evil laugh. Don't you?"

And, throwing back his head, Barbu let out a long, dreadful cackle that chilled the spines of all who heard it. Oh! He is ROTTEN.

Wilma had scrunched the morning paper into a ball and thrown it into the nearest trash can. "What a load of rubbish, Pickle!" she moaned.

"They don't know what they're talking about! This hullabaloo is out of control. Everyone's gone hysterical and I haven't the time or enough hands to shake, shout at, or slap them all!" She sighed and uncrossed her arms. Climbing out of bed, she wandered over to the open sack she had picked up from Madam Skratch.

Taking the box from the sack, she emptied its contents onto the floor. Pickle, who was dealing with a deep and persistent itch in his left ear, had yet to give everything a good sniff. Now that he was an apprentice detective's dog, he had duties too, but right at that precise moment, with his foot stuck in his ear, he couldn't quite be as useful as he might be.

Wilma crouched down onto the back of her heels and stared at the letters in front of her. They were addressed to Madam Skratch and all had the same mysterious heading: With regard to Child 472.

"Child four seventy-two?" Wilma whispered, pursing her lips together in thought. "I suppose that must be me." She picked up the letter nearest to her and read, "'Madam Skratch, enclosed three grogs. Upkeep. June. Yours sincerely' . . . Can't quite make out the name," Wilma added, turning the letter sideways and squinting. "But someone cared enough to cover my upkeep."

Pickle scratched on. It really was a relentless itch.

It's at this point that the Cooper monetary system should be explained. Most countries have their own currency. In the United Kingdom, for example, the citizens carry notes and coins called pounds and pence. Sometimes, grown-ups will hand children pence or, if they are very lucky, pounds and encourage them to stuff these into pottery pigs. On Cooper, the citizens have neither coins nor notes. Instead they have a pebble system called grogs and groggles. So there are seventy-six groggles to a grog, eighty-two grogs to a mega-grog, and thirty-one mega-grogs to a ginorma-grog. There is nothing bigger than a ginorma-grog, which is a good thing, as they are extremely difficult to carry. Cooper adults also encourage their children to stuff grogs into pigs. But on Cooper the pigs are real, which inevitably leads to enormous vet bills. At present there are no exchange rates for grogs and groggles. But this is because no one has ever been to Cooper. And no one from Cooper has ever left. So that's that explained. Let's get back to the story.

"Most of these letters just say the same thing," explained Wilma to Pickle, who was now rubbing his ear up against the leg of Wilma's bed. "It's always three grogs, but for loads of different months."

As Wilma began to pile the letters into date order, Pickle, with some relief, finally managed to dispatch the itch. It had been caused by a rather tenacious earwig that had crawled into Pickle's ear and knitted itself a nest out of dog hair. Still, he'd managed to dislodge it and send the insect packing. Finally he could turn his thoughts to a loftier plain: namely, smelling stuff.

And something on the floor in front of Wilma was *fascinating* him. It was a thick, meaty odor, the sort of smell that a small beagle could be driven wild by. With his nose to the ground he snuffled through the still-to-be-sorted letters.

No, it wasn't there. Perhaps it was coming from the top of Wilma's half-scrunched sock? No. Not there either. And then, turning his head sharply to his left, a deep, penetrating stink wafted up Pickle's nostrils. Oh heaven! Whatever it was, it was wonderfully awful and it was coming from the strange piece of material that Wilma had found in with her letters. He *had* to roll in it.

"Pickle!" cried out Wilma as her naughty beagle dived toward the dirty white piece of material, scattering her already sorted letters everywhere. With his legs in the air and his tongue lolling out, Pickle rolled as if his life depended on it.

Wilma stared down at the small scene of devastation. "I'm quite cross with you," she chided as Pickle eventually allowed himself to be pulled up and off. "I am trying to be methodical. And you're not helping."

But Pickle didn't care. He stank too now. And he was full of himself.

"Ewww!" said Wilma suddenly as she picked up the mysterious scrap of material that Pickle had just vacated. "That stinks!" The smell, Wilma discovered, was emanating from a dark, indefinable smear on the square cloth. There was also a picture in one of the corners of a pair of crossed meat chops. "Such a strange fabric for a baby blanket!" she added as she held it at arm's length. "It's so thin. It can't have been warm. Perhaps if we send some of it to Penbert she can analyze it for results? What do you think, Pickle?"

He didn't answer. He was still lost in an odor-based reverie.

After cutting out a small square from the stained piece of material and putting it into a Clue Bag, Wilma returned to her original task. All the letters seemed the same and the name of the sender was always indecipherable, but then, just as she was about to give up and go down for breakfast, her hand fell upon a lone letter that was written in a different handwriting and had no reference to Child 472 on it.

"This must be the letter that Madam Skratch told me about," Wilma whispered. "The one she was sent just before I left the Institute . . ." As she began to read, her heart started to thump faster.

To whomsoever it might concern,

I wonder if you can be of assistance. Many years ago a child was delivered to your Institute. She was six weeks of age and had blond wayward hair that would never quite stick down. Her eyes were green and her face had a cheeky aspect. I have reason to believe that she may have been my sister's daughter. The child was left with someone who may have delivered her to the Institute for Woeful Children. I understand that most orphans or mislaid children end up there. I am sure a lot of children are left with you so to jog your memory I can tell you that there was a particularly bad storm on the night the child went missing. Perhaps I

Wilma turned the paper over to read the rest, but the back page was blank. "Oh no," she said, frantically searching through the remaining letters. "Madam Skratch was right. The burned second page means there's no address and no signature.

It's just like the case we're investigating with Mr. Goodman. Another missing bit of paper!"

Wilma's mind whirred with possibilities. Someone had been looking for her. Was the sister the letter spoke of her mother? Was the letter from an aunt or uncle? And who had sent the other letters? And why? The money had stopped being sent when she left the Institute. Someone somewhere was watching her! But who? And where from? Somehow she had to find out! The door to her room was flung open. It was Mrs. Speckle.

"Wilma!" she exclaimed, sounding a little choked. "Something terrible has happened." The housekeeper wiped something from her face. Then, with a deep sniff, she looked back up at Wilma and said, "Mr. Goodman is gone."

"Gone?" Wilma asked. "Up to the Valiant? Or to the lab? Or to see Inspector Lemone?"

"No," answered Mrs. Speckle, getting out her knitted handkerchief and blowing into it. "He has gone. Hounded away! Chased off! He went in the night. Left me a note. There's one for you too. Here."

Her hand shaking, Wilma reached for the folded paper with her name on it.

Dear Wilma,

There comes a time in every detective's life when they have to make decisions that they think are for the best. My presence is jeopardizing the case (if you don't know what jeopardizing means, look it up but, by way of a clue, it means making things a bit wobbly) and so I think it is best for all concerned if I commit myself to what we detectives call a period of "lying low." As my apprentice, I would like you to help Inspector Lemone as much as you can. You've already uncovered plenty of clues. And there are lots of suspects. Keep your wits about you, Wilma. The killer could strike again at any moment. I won't be far away, but for now I must remain hidden.

Think logically.

I remain,
Theodore P. Goodman

The note fell from Wilma's hand.

A detective vanished in the night? Four people dead and a ten-year-old left in charge? Does anyone else think that's a good idea? No? Didn't think so.

"**B**ut I always ride in the back," said Inspector Lemone anxiously. "What I mean to say is Goodman did the steering. Perhaps we should walk?"

"Or run," suggested Wilma. "We could do that."

Inspector Lemone looked down at the ten-year-old and blinked hard. "Run? Don't be ridiculous."

Wilma, realizing that Inspector Lemone was even more confused than she was, thought again. "Well, you could go in the cart at the back of the tandem. Pickle and I could ride it. Although, having said that, I'm not sure his paws will reach the pedals. Or I could sit in Mr. Goodman's seat in the front. But, to be honest, my sense of direction isn't that brilliant . . ."

"This is a fine mess," declared the Inspector, mopping his brow with his handkerchief. "Goodman vanishes. Tandem needs riding. Well, there's nothing for it. I shall have to sit in Goodman's seat after all. Have we got enough food? In case of emergencies?"

"I've given you a box of twenty corn crumbles, Inspector," said Mrs. Speckle, handing him a small knapsack. "And a flask of peppermint tea. Just in case."

The Inspector's face softened. Experiencing the sweet flush of devotion that coursed through him whenever Mrs. Speckle was near, he stared down at the floor and gulped.

Wilma rolled her eyes. "The Valiant is only a quarter of a mile away, Inspector Lemone. I think we'll be all right," she said, climbing onto the back seat of the tandem. "We must press on. It's what Mr. Goodman would have wanted."

The Inspector gave himself a brisk shake at the sound of his missing friend's name. "You're right, Wilma. We must proceed as he would want us to. Ought to get on. Okay. Front seat. What's that? Ooooh! Bell. Best leave that alone. The Valiant! Here we come!"

The Inspector and Wilma began pedaling as fast as they could, but mysteriously they weren't actually moving. After a quick think, Wilma stood up on her pedals and tapped the Inspector on the shoulder.

"Strangest thing!" he shouted, glancing back. "Can't figure it out!"

"Hand brake," she answered, pointing down.

"So it is," replied the Inspector, a little embarrassed. And, with a swift release, off they shot.

Thankfully for all concerned, the road to the Valiant was an easy one. Wilma was able to stop on the way and mail a package with the scrap of fabric in it to Penbert and, despite a small incident with one of the Sugarcane Swizzle dispensing taps, the journey proved relatively successful.

Pickle, whose goggles, as a result of this slight collision, were full of Sugarcane Swizzle fizz, was less pleased with the journey than his companions, but that wasn't surprising, given the sticky circumstances.

"Quite out of breath," panted Inspector Lemone as he dismounted at last. "Still, at least we got here in one piece."

The tandem had pulled up just outside the stage door to the rear of the Valiant and as Wilma helped Pickle out of the cart and emptied his goggles of fizz an old man with a broom appeared. He was wearing a torn pair of trousers, a grubby striped shirt covered by a knitted waistcoat full of holes, and a cap so large that his face was virtually hidden except for an enormous gray-flecked beard that hung almost to the center of his chest. "Can't park that there," he muttered, wagging a finger. "No, no!"

Inspector Lemone turned and frowned. "Of course we can leave it here," he blustered. "We always leave it here."

"And you can't stay here either!" added the

old man, pushing his broom toward them. "Mr. D'Anvers likes the place tidy!"

"Well, you can tell Mr. D'Anvers that we are here on official business and we shall make the place as untidy as we see fit!" retorted Inspector Lemone, pushing his chest out.

"'Scuse me, 'scuse me," the old man went on, sweeping around their feet as he pushed past them to the stage door. "If you want to clean up properly," he added, bending low as he reached for the handle, "you have to look even for what's not there!" And into the Valiant he vanished.

Inspector Lemone blinked. "Silly old fool," he muttered. "Just the sort of fellow Barbu D'Anvers would have working for him! Now then. Let's think. We're here. And we've got to do stuff . . . and then . . . hmm."

Wilma looked up at her friend. He was blinking a lot, which she knew meant his brain was in a spin. "I think I might need a few of those emergency corn crumbles," he mumbled. "They are very good during moments of stress."

"I'm trying to work out what Mr. Goodman

would do," said Wilma, passing him the knapsack of biscuits. "Thinking about that playbill, he'd probably want to work out what, and where, the missing bit is. So I think we should investigate that first."

The Inspector, shoving three corn crumbles into his mouth at once, nodded. "Capital idea," he answered. "I'll start with that ventriloquist, Mrs. Wanderlip. Leave it to me! I'm very good at calm questioning under dire circumstances . . ."

"DIE!" screamed Eric Ohio, arms flapping, five minutes later. "We're going to DIE! And she's letting him make us go on!"

"There, there," spluttered Inspector Lemone desperately as he was being sprayed with jetting tears. "I must say you seem to be taking this a lot better than your . . . um . . . dummy, Mrs. Wanderlip."

"He's at the end of his tether, Inspector," explained the ventriloquist as Eric's eyes popped out on stalks. "But this is our job. And we have to eat. We've got no choice. The show must go on.

It's worrying but . . . what choice do we have?"

"Worrying?" screamed Eric Ohio, his hat shooting upward. "We're going to DIE and all you can say is that it's worrying?"

Wilma, who had been staring at Eric's missing finger, sensed an opportunity. "What happened to your hand, Eric?" she said, pointing as nonchalantly as she could.

"Vandalized! Abused!" screamed the dummy, his head rotating. "It's a warning, I tell you! We're next!"

"Actually," whispered Mrs. Wanderlip, patting Eric on the forearm, "I don't know what happened. I left him alone in our dressing room, came back, it was gone."

Wilma twitched her nose. She needed to be careful not to reveal her thoughts, like Mr. Goodman had taught her. Could she believe Mrs. Wanderlip? Had someone stolen Eric's finger? Mr. Goodman did seem to think that the murderer was trying to frame people. Perhaps this was another clue? She'd have to think about that later.

"Mrs. Wanderlip," said Wilma, continuing

with her questioning. "Have a look at the playbill. There's a bit at the bottom that's been ripped off. Can you remember what might have been there?"

She shook her head. "It was so long ago . . ." she began. "Playbills just list the acts that are on that night."

"That must be it!" Wilma's eyes widened. "There must have been someone else on the bill! Another act! Think, Mrs. Wanderlip! Who else was onstage that night?"

"Good question," said the Inspector, reaching for a fourth biscuit. "Wish I'd thought of it."

"Wait," began Mrs. Wanderlip, forehead condensing with frown lines. "Now that I think about it . . . I can't seem to . . ."

"Shut up!" chipped in Eric Ohio, her irascible dummy. "Leave this to me! I remember. There was a novelty act on that night. Can't remember what exactly, but it was odd, unusual. Wore a mask. Anyway, it all failed. It was horrendous. Got laughed off the stage. Made the show look terrible. Made us all look terrible! We were outraged. Especially Cecily."

"And can you remember the act's name?" pressed Wilma, urging the dummy on.

Eric's head rattled a little around his collar. "Mysterious Mezmo!" he announced, legs flipping upward. "That was it! Mysterious Mezmo!"

"Oh my goodness," said Wilma gulping. "We've found a proper clue, Inspector Lemone. All on our own."

"I know," said the Inspector, reaching for a handkerchief to wipe his forehead. "It's all a little overwhelming."

"'Scuse me, 'scuse me," said the cleaner, appearing suddenly from the shadows and pushing his way past them. "It's all change here. Mark my words! All change!"

"Be off with you!" snapped the Inspector, spitting crumbs. "We're conducting proper detective business!"

The cleaner pulled down his cap and shuffled off, muttering.

"And can you tell us what Mezmo looked like?" Wilma went on, ignoring the interruption.

"Have you got cloth for ears?" snapped Eric

Ohio, his head rotating. "I just told you! Mezmo wore a mask!"

Wilma excitedly reached for her apprentice detective notebook. "I'm writing this ALL down, Inspector. I think it might be very important."

Inspector Lemone, flushed with their small success, stuck his chest out and cleared his throat. "And this Mezmo . . . happen to know where they are now?"

Mrs. Wanderlip shook her head. "No. Never saw or heard of the act again."

"So maybe *that's* why the name's been ripped off, Wilma," opined Inspector Lemone, tapping his hands behind his back. "No need to bump someone off if they're not still around."

"Hmm," pondered Wilma, "you might be right. Or . . ."

But just then the creak she had heard twice before in such incriminating circumstances sounded behind them. Wilma swung around and gasped. It was Gorgeous Muldoon. He was walking toward them, face contorted, and with every step there was the telltale creak.

"You all right?" asked Inspector Lemone, seeing that the comedian was in some discomfort.

"New shoes," Gorgeous muttered as he sloughed past. "They're agony."

Wilma looked down at Pickle, her eyes wide with excitement. Was Gorgeous Muldoon the killer after all? Was he? If Wilma was going to find out, she had to come up with a plan. And fast.

"It was definitely the same creak, Inspector!" Wilma urged as they made their way to the foyer. "The same one I heard before Sylvester died AND before I got hit on the noggin! Maybe you're right and the Mysterious Mezmo thing is just a wild-duck chase?"

"Goose chase," corrected the Inspector. "Or is it chicken? No. Wait. It is goose. As you were."

"Maybe it's like the Case of the Gargling Gardener? When Mr. Goodman realized that he was chasing the wrong man? We mustn't make that mistake. It's important for me to show I'm learning. It has to be Gorgeous Muldoon!" continued Wilma. "He's probably doing it for Cecily! Just like Loranda said! I really think we should do that thing that detectives do."

"Yes, we should!" the Inspector declared, before adding, "Sorry . . . remind me. What is that exactly?"

"You know!" replied Wilma, jumping up and down. "When they make their inquiries go all concentrated! It's in my Academy textbook! You follow one suspect about. It's called tightening the net!"

"Oh!" declared Inspector Lemone with considerable relief. "Tightening the net! Yes. I have actually heard of that. So that's good. Though is that a real net? I'm terribly bad at sewing."

"No. A detective's net. Which is invisible. Hang on. I'll find the bit we need . . ." Wilma reached into her pinafore pocket.

Tightening the Net

Sometimes, a crime has a range of suspects. And, during the course of an investigation, one suspect may become more suspicious than others. At this point, detectives should consider tightening the net, a method by which a closer eye can be kept on the suspect in question and further clues gathered. When keeping a closer eye on suspects, it's best not to be too conspicuous. So going undercover is recommended.

Wilma tucked her book away once more, her face deep in thought. "Perhaps we could go undercover, Pickle? As a cat? Or a rat?"

Pickle shot Wilma a dismissive glance. There was no way he was being a cat. No way, no how.

"All right then," said Inspector Lemone with a small gulp. "I'll follow Gorgeous around a bit. Keep a tight eye on him. Maybe you should go back to the cottage? Ask Mrs. Speckle to make some sandwiches. We might be here for a while. In fact, yes, that's best. We're in this for the long haul. So off you go. And maybe bring a few pies as well. And a sponge cake . . . just to be safe."

As she ran off, Wilma was filled with a sense of purpose. Here they were, on their own and on the verge of cracking a case, just like Mr. Goodman! Her mind was whirring. She'd run back to Clarissa Cottage, get the sandwiches and—

Wilma stopped in her tracks. There, hanging above the entrance of the theatre was a new sign being hung in place by Janty.

FRIGHT NIGHT TRY-OUTS!
NEW ACTS REQUIRED!
TOMORROW AT THE
D'ANVERS VAU-DEVIL!

"D'Anvers Vau-Devil?" she scoffed, squinting upward. "I can't believe it. He's named the theatre after himself!"

"And why shouldn't he?" retorted Janty, jumping down from his ladder. "He is in charge. It's nice having a boss who knows what he's doing. Oh . . . but then I'm forgetting . . . you wouldn't know what *that* was like."

"Mr. Goodman knows what he's doing more than anyone I've ever met," snapped Wilma, determined to defend her mentor.

221

"Really?" answered Janty, looking about him in an exaggerated manner. "Then where is he? Afraid to show his face, I expect."

Wilma bit her lip. Her insides were boiling with rage. She knew that she ought to rise above it, like Mr. Goodman would want her to, but this was more than she could bear. Janty, seeing that he'd upset her, sneered with pleasure. But his face suddenly changed to one of horror. He looked down at his leg. Pickle, who had had just about enough of this young boy, had taken matters into his own paws, cocked his leg, and peed into Janty's sock.

"Sorry," said Wilma with a small shrug. "I think he was desperate."

Janty hopped off in disgust, and Wilma added, "I suppose I should be angry with you for that, Pickle." They turned and walked away. "But for some reason I can't bring myself to. Can you believe that boy? He's getting worse by the day. And can you believe Barbu is advertising for new acts? But hang on! That's it," she said, snapping her fingers. "That's how we can catch Gorgeous!

I'll go undercover as a new vaudeville act! Using a disguise can sometimes be cunning! That's one of the top tips, remember? And actually, Pickle, we should keep it quiet from the Inspector. That way we can really keep things secret. And, besides, it might be a bit dangerous, and you know how the Inspector hates me doing anything like that."

Pickle snorted. He didn't much care for doing dangerous things either.

Keeping Inspector Lemone in the dark was going to be a risk. But, as much as she respected him, Wilma knew that the Inspector had a tendency to be clumsy and she couldn't afford to have her cover blown by one small accidental comment. Instead, she would give instructions to Mrs. Speckle to tell the Inspector that she had gone off to see if Penbert had any more results. That way, her secret would be safe.

"I'm going to be Maude Muddle and her Amazing Cat Pizzazz. Pickle's going to be the cat. Aren't you, Pickle?" said Wilma, explaining her new plan to Mrs. Speckle, having arrived back at Clarissa

Cottage. Pickle, who was enduring having some triangular pieces of toast stuck to the top of his head, was in no mood to respond. "Those will be his cat ears," continued Wilma, pointing. "Although they need to be less toasty and more furry."

Mrs. Speckle, who hadn't really been herself since Theodore's departure and seemed to be spending all her time knitting a pipe "to remember him by," glanced up. "What's your act?" she asked, clearing her throat a little. "You can't just have a name. You need to have an act."

"Oh," said Wilma, inadvertently eating one of Pickle's ears. "I don't really know. If it helps, Pickle can't sing. And neither can I. At least I don't think I can . . ."

Wilma stood up, closed her eyes, and let rip. "A braaiiin! Braaaaiiin! Braaaaaiiin! It makes meeeeeethaaaaaaaane! 'Cuz it's a braaaaaaain!"

Mrs. Speckle blinked. "No," she said finally. "You definitely can't."

"Hmm," sighed Wilma. "I wonder what we can do."

Mrs. Speckle took off her knitted spectacles and looked down at Wilma. "Not a lot of people know this," she began with a small swallow, "but in my younger days I did a little vaudeville myself."

Wilma's eyes widened. "Did you?" she asked, suitably surprised.

"I was in a dance troupe. But they moved into tap dancing and my knitted boots didn't really fit the bill. Still! That's behind me now! All the same, I can teach you everything you need to know about vaudeville."

Wilma beamed. "Really? What shall we start with?"

"Basic Grins and Grimaces," said Mrs. Speckle, rolling up her cardigan sleeves. "And then we shall progress to Theatrical Flimflam!"

"Thank you!" said Wilma, readying herself for her lesson. "The open auditions are tomorrow morning, so we need to get a move on. I just hope we can work something out in time. You know, so Mr. Goodman would be pleased."

Mrs. Speckle, who was not known for her kindness, especially where small, determined girls and their cheeky dogs were concerned, took a deep breath. "Yes," she mumbled gruffly.

225

"Seeing as it's for Mr. Goodman." Mrs. Speckle adjusted her double bobble hats. She may present a grumpy aspect. But she's all right really.

Wilma and Pickle were up all night, during which Wilma had discovered, quite by accident, that Pickle could dance. "Who knew?" she said as, with the help of Mrs. Speckle, a dance routine was whipped into shape. They were exhausted and aching but when dawn finally arrived, they were ready.

"Now don't forget!" shouted Mrs. Speckle as Wilma and Pickle set off for the auditions. "Kick, turn, spin, kick, shimmy, shimmy, jazz hands!"

"We won't!" yelled back Wilma, throwing a bag with their costumes over her shoulder.

Because Wilma knew the Inspector would be on his way to the cottage for his breakfast, she and Pickle had to carry their costumes away from the house to a quiet spot to get changed before arriving at the theatre. A couple of streets away, in an empty alley, Wilma quickly laced Pickle into a pink tutu and finished the outfit with a small coned hat, on either side of which sat his toast ears. Wilma was to be dressed as a clown using a baggy, polka-dot pair of dungarees sewn to an old shirt that Mrs. Speckle had cut to size and finished off the collar with a frilly trim. She had crocheted Wilma a red wig too and completed the outfit with a large pair of white padded garden gloves. Now, to make her disguise even more cunning, Wilma made herself a false red nose from putty and smeared thick greasepaint, a special actor's makeup, over her face. She was totally unrecognizable.

"Remember, Pickle, you're a cat. So put on a few airs and graces and don't look pleased to see anybody."

Pickle just snorted. He would do anything Wilma asked of him but, lest we forget, our favorite noble hound was dressed in a ballet outfit and had to pretend to be a cat. He was putting on a brave face, but by golly, he was *dying* inside.

To Wilma's surprise, the line for the auditions snaked out from the foyer and down the street. There were barrel jumpers, harpists, a man with a harmonica hidden inside a sandwich, roller skaters, gun spinners, trick cyclists, whip experts, and a man in swimming trunks claiming he could hold his breath underwater for five whole minutes. "Goodness," said Wilma as she surveyed the scene. "I can't believe there are so many people here. Especially as there's a killer on the loose in the theatre. Still, some people will do anything to be in show business! We're going to have to give this our all, Pickle. Don't forget the jazz hands. Mrs. Speckle says they're crucial."

Baron von Worms, who seemed a little overwhelmed by the numbers of auditioners, was standing on the theatre steps with a clipboard. Since being ousted as manager he had been forced by Barbu to do all kinds of menial jobs.

"No! I'm sorry!" he was saying to a tall woman dressed like a carrot. "We already have a paper tearer! No thank you! Next!"

Wilma, thinking that this would be a perfect way to test out their disguise, walked past the line and approached him.

"Helloo," she said, throwing in an accent for

extra cunning. "Me cat 'n' I would like to try out for the show!"

The Baron looked down at them over the top of his clipboard. "Name?" he said without batting an eyelid.

Wilma trilled inwardly. Her disguise was working! "I'm Maude Muddle," she explained. "And this heere's me cat. He's deeefinitely a cat. His name's Pizzazz. So that's me, Maude Muddle, and me amaaazin' dog, I mean cat, Pizzazz!"

"Very large for a cat, isn't he?" commented the Baron, eyeing Pickle up and down.

"That's 'cuz he doesn't eat mice," answered Wilma, thinking on her feet, "he eats raats!"

"Hmph." Baron von Worms shrugged, scribbling on his clipboard. "Well, that would explain it. There are rats the size of pigs around the back of the Valiant."

"D'Anvers! Not Valiant!" corrected Barbu sharply as he swept past them. "Do try and get it right, Mr. von Worms!"

"It's Baron . . ." muttered the set-upon manager. But it was too late. The tiny rotter was already gone.

"Send the first one in, would you?" said Janty, sauntering up the front steps. He stopped and stared at Wilma. His eyes narrowed. Wilma's heart thumped. If she was discovered now, the plan would be in shreds! "I like your wig," he said eventually with a wonky grin and then, stuffing his hands into his pockets, he followed his master into the theatre. She had done it! If she could fool Janty, she could fool anyone!

"Well, he approves!" sniffed the Baron, handing Wilma a scrap of paper. "Which is a start. In fact," he added, twirling his pen, "you can go in first! Best to keep D'Anvers and his crew in a good mood. Off you go. Up the stairs, turn left, into the stalls, pop up onto the stage."

"Thank you!" called out Wilma as she and Pickle scampered off.

"And be good!" shouted the Baron, watching them go. "Or they'll make my life even more of a misery. Right, then. Next!"

Barbu, Tully, and Janty were all sitting on the stage behind a long table, goblets of water before them. The old man that Wilma had seen the previous day was sweeping up around their feet while Geoffrey was on his hands and knees painting a large X on the floor in front of the judges' table. Malcolm Poppledore, the props boy, was standing at the foot of the stage and on seeing Wilma, he took the slip of paper she'd been given at the entrance, cleared his throat, and shouted up, "First contestant, Mr. D'Anvers. Maude Muddle and her Amazing Cat Pizzazz!"

"Ugh," moaned Barbu, giving Tully a nudge. "Animal act."

"I quite like animals, Mr. Barbu," replied the stupid henchman. "They don't think much."

"Figures," sneered the evil villain. "So! Maude Muddle! Up onto the stage, please. Stand on the X. And, in your own time, blah, blah, blah, tell us about yourself!"

Wilma looked down at Pickle and whispered behind her hand, "Now for the theatrical flim-flam! Just follow my lead and look a bit miserable." Turning to the judges, she clutched her hands together, just as Mrs. Speckle had taught her, and took a small step forward. "Me and me cat," she began in a quiet hush, "'ave bin through goood times. But we also been through baaad. Especially Pizzazz. He 'ad a twin who loved to dance. But one day his twin was walking past an orphanage on fire. With no thought for his own personal safety, his twin went into that fire and saved every laaaaast orphan in there."

"Amazing," muttered Tully, hanging on to Wilma's every word.

"But the thing was," Wilma continued, letting her head hang low, "on his last trip in, he was struck by a flaming beam and he went lame. He would never daaance again."

"Oh no!" whispered Tully, his hand rushing to his mouth.

"And Pizzazz here," Wilma added, gesturing down to Pickle, who was, rather brilliantly, lying on the floor with his paws over his eyes, "swore that he would learn to dance for his lame brother. And that's why we're here today."

Wilma looked up dramatically as Mrs. Speckle had shown her. All the judges were staring at her, openmouthed and silent. Tully was in tears, Janty was frowning, and even Barbu, the hardest-hearted man on Cooper Island, was looking a little choked up. Eventually, he spoke.

"That's quite a story, Maude Muddle," he said softly. "Well, let's see this dance. And let's see if Pizzazz can honor his lame hero brother."

This was it. The moment for which they had worked tirelessly through the night. Wilma handed her sheet music to the pianist and, taking up position, she waited for the first notes to begin. Side by side, Wilma and Pickle began to nod their heads in time to the music. Then Wilma, snapping her fingers, slid sideways and struck a pose as Pickle shimmied his rear end and took center stage, his twinkling tutu catching the light magnificently. To the amazement of the judges, the grooving cat kicked his back legs out, spun around, shook his rear end toward them as if his life depended on it, rolled onto his back and pedaled his paws upward in time to the music. At this point, Wilma jumped in the air, then, jiggling like jelly, pulled a large knitted mouse out of her pocket. Tossing it over to Pickle, who caught it, patted it, and then tore it to shreds, Wilma got down on all fours and crawled forward. Pickle, who was trying his best to twitch his tail just like the cat they had saved from the pear tree, jumped, in one startling springing movement, onto Wilma's shoulders. With his head directly above Wilma's they rolled their necks and turned left, then right and then in one snappy move they both looked upward at the same time. Pickle jumped down and Wilma leaped up. In perfect time, they kicked their legs, turned, spun, kicked again, and then shimmied their shoulders forward, and finally, in one fabulous movement, Pickle stood up on his hind legs and as Wilma shook her hands from side to side, Pickle did the same with his front paws.

"Oh!" said Barbu, practically breathless. "Jazz hands! I LOVE them!"

The routine was over. It had been a triumph. Wilma smiled down at Pickle, who, even though he was dressed like a cat, was experiencing the sweet rush of adrenaline that dancing brings. Surely they would get through! Surely!

"Well," began Janty, "I think the routine needs a little sharpening through the midsection, but . . . I loved it. It's a yes from me."

Wilma looked toward Tully. He was clapping and crying simultaneously. "Yes! Yes! Yes!" he bawled. "One million percent yes!"

It was looking good. But they needed Barbu to agree. Without his say-so, the plan was dead in the water. The tiny villain sat back in his chair and sucked his cheeks in thought. "Do you know what?" he said eventually. "It's . . . three yeses! You're in!"

Wilma and Pickle had done it! Let the choir of angels sing!

"**T**his is your dressing room," bustled Malcolm Poppledore, opening a door into a tiny, cramped space. "You did well. They didn't hire a single other act today. So you're the only new one on the bill. The next show starts in an hour. Running order will be stage left. Do you have any props I need to organize?"

"No thank you," replied Wilma, turning up the gaslights around the mirror. "Although a bowl of water for Pizzazz might be nice."

"Water?" answered Malcolm, staring down at Pickle. "That's a bit mean. Don't cats prefer milk?"

"Yes. Okay," blurted Wilma, backtracking. "Must be all the excitement of getting the job. In that case, make it creamy! Ah-ha-ha. Ha."

Pickle rolled his eyes. He hated milk. It made him bloaty and, to be honest, even though he slightly loathed his tutu, he still wanted to look good in it.

"All right then," said Malcolm, who was in too much of a rush to notice anything properly. "I'll bring around fresh greasepaints in half an hour."

A large thud sounded against the wall behind the mirror, followed by the muffled yells of Cecily Lovely.

Malcolm sighed. "Cecily's off again," he muttered. "That dresser of hers deserves a medal. You'll soon find out. What with being next door to her dressing room and everything. My advice—keep out of her way. Unless you want something thrown at you too."

As Malcolm left, Wilma looked around the dressing room. There were two mirrors, two chairs, and a few threadbare posters on the walls. In the corner there was a rack to hang costumes on and a pile of discarded pots of greasepaint remover. "Not very comfy, is it, Pickle?" commented Wilma. "Still, so far so good. Our undercover plan is working brilliantly. What we need to do now is track down Gorgeous Muldoon and follow him around a bit. In case he gets more suspicious. And, if he does, collect clues and make a net out of them. Or something."

"Are you Maude Muddle?" said a voice from the doorway. It was Mrs. Grumbletubs, the laundry mistress. She looked anxious and a little distracted.

"Yes," replied Wilma with a grin. "And this is my amaaazing cat Pizzazz. He's amaaazing."

Mrs. Grumbletubs cast a glance at Pickle, who, at that precise moment, was trying to eat a slightly moldy apple core that he'd found on the dressing table. "Do you have any costumes you need washing or ironing?" she asked, pressing on. "Can't really stop. Mind so full. Terrible deaths. Washing and ironing. Always washing and ironing. So awful. Wish I hadn't seen it. But I have. But I can't tell! I've my son to think about!"

Wilma, sensing that Mrs. Grumbletubs was in something of a state, stepped forward and placed a comforting hand on her forearm. "Are you all right?" she asked, giving her false nose a twitch. "Do you know something about the deaths?"

"Fizzing and frothing! No! Said too much. Mustn't tell. Not safe! No one's safe!" mumbled the laundry mistress, wringing her hands together.

"Frothing?" asked Wilma, a small surge of excitement shooting through her. "Do you mean the poison? Do you know how it works? Do you know where it's coming from?"

The door to Wilma's dressing room was slightly ajar and at that moment Pickle looked up from his very dissatisfying snack to see a shadow moving across the door frame. Leaping off his chair he stood, stiff as a board and paw aloft, and barked at the shadow.

Mrs. Grumbletubs frowned. "I thought you said he was a cat?"

"He is," explained Wilma quickly, a little irritated at her beagle's interruption. "But he can do dog impressions. I told you he was amaaazing. Anyway, never mind that—the poison—you said you knew something!"

Pickle barked again. He had to make Wilma understand! He turned, pawed at her leg, and then barked again in the direction of the shadow. At last Wilma followed his gaze and she saw it. A dark shape lingering behind the half-closed door.

"Gorgeous Muldoon," she whispered, and lunging for the door handle she pulled it toward her! "Caught you!" she yelled as the door flung open.

"Oh!" said Scraps, jumping. "Sorry! Didn't mean to startle you! I've got a pile of costumes for Mrs. Grumbletubs," she added, gesturing with her nose to the huge heap of clothes in her arms. "Thought I'd wait till you were done. So as not to be rude. I'm Scraps. I work for Miss Lovely."

"Oh!" said Wilma with a sigh of relief. "I thought you were . . . Well, never mind that now. I'm Maude Muddle. This is Pizzazz. He's a caaat, but sometimes he pretends to be a dog. Can I help with those? They look quite heavy!"

"Thank you, yes," answered Scraps with a weak smile. "Miss Lovely does have an awful lot of clothes. And she likes to change her outfit every thirty minutes to stay fashionable, so, you know."

As Wilma helped the poor dresser put the sequined outfits and flowing frocks into Mrs. Grumbletubs's laundry basket, the troubled washerwoman was still muttering under her breath.

"All done, Mrs. Grumbletubs," said Wilma as the last feather boa was stuffed in with the rest of the laundry. "Perhaps I'll come and see you later. We can finish that chat we were having."

But Mrs. Grumbletubs was already making for the door, basket in her arms and shaking her head as she went. "Terrible times! Said too much! Too much!" And with that she was gone.

"Mrs. Grumbletubs seems very upset," observed Scraps, dusting a loose feather from her dungarees. "But then we all are. It's been a trying time. What was she saying?"

"Oh, nothing much," said Wilma quickly with a shrug. Detectives always save what they're thinking till last, of course, and it certainly wouldn't do for Wilma to start spouting on about potential clues. An awkward silence filled the room. You may have noticed grown-ups have a lot of these. Especially when gentlemen have made improper comments about ladies' new hairdos. In these circumstances it is vital to change the subject, and fast, which is exactly what Wilma did now.

"Do you mind me asking?" she said, staring at Scraps's hands. "I couldn't help noticing. Everyone's alwaaays wearing gloves. Is it a theatre thing?"

"Oh!" replied Scraps with a small raise of her eyebrows. "Most people wear them because the place is so dusty, but I have to wear them because I can't touch greasepaint. Bad luck, I know! I work in a theatre and I'm allergic to actor's makeup! And boot polish. In fact I'm allergic to practically everything! Which is a pain because I'm always having to make up Miss Lovely's beauty preparations."

"SCRAAAAAAAAAAPS!" came a yell from the adjacent dressing room.

"I'd better go," Scraps said softly. "Miss Lovely wants me. But it was nice to meet you. And your cat."

Wilma blinked. When she had read the chapter in her book about going undercover, there had been a paragraph about establishing confidences and working with people with insider know-how. Scraps might be perfect! She was always with Miss Lovely, and Gorgeous Muldoon was always hanging around *her*! Besides, Wilma liked Scraps and considered her a friend. She was sure it was something Theodore P. Goodman would do. In fact, he'd sort of suggested as much when he asked Wilma to quiz Scraps about Cecily. Whichever way she looked at it, it was a flawless idea.

"Um, Scraps," she began, reaching out and stopping the dresser from leaving. "The thing is . . ." she added, dropping her accent, "we've met before."

Scraps spun around. "I don't think we have," she replied stiffly. "I'm sure I'd remember—I remember everyone I've met. You must have me mistaken for someone else. Please excuse me. I have to clean out the Countess's bins."

"No, Scraps!" urged Wilma, her eyes widening. "It's me! Wilma Tenderfoot. And that's not Pizzazz! It's Pickle! He's just pretending to be a cat. Look! He's got toast for ears! I'm wearing a false nose!" She gave her putty nose a tweak. "I'm undercover. On official apprentice detective business! Nobody knows it's me!"

Scraps looked slightly taken aback. A small, troubled expression flitted across her face. "But . . ." she began, "if you're in disguise, why are you telling me?"

"You can help me!" enthused the ten-year-old. "You can be my Man on the Inside! That's the proper term. I read about it in my book. Although you're not a man. But then, it didn't say you had to be. And you have got insider know-how! You can look out for fishy goings-on and help me make a net of clues!"

"I'm just a d-dresser," stuttered Scraps, backing toward the door. "I'm not sure I'm the right person."

"You are! You're perfect!" encouraged Wilma. "Here's the thing. Oh, hang on. Before I tell you anything, you sort of have to promise not to say a word. Put your finger on my apprentice badge and swear it. It's here, hidden under this knitted daffodil."

Scraps placed a finger gingerly on the small, shiny badge. "All right, I promise. What . . . what do you know?"

"Here's the thing. Two times I heard a strange creaky noise. And then I found out that it was coming from Gorgeous Muldoon's new shoes!"

Scraps bit her lip nervously.

"There are lots of other clues too, but Gorgeous is definitely the Prime Suspect. Now we just have to catch him doing something so suspicious that Inspector Lemone can arrest him and Mr. Goodman can come back from his hiding place."

"Theodore P. Goodman has gone into hiding?" gasped Scraps. "I wondered where he was . . ."

"Don't worry. I've sort of been left in charge. This case will be solved in no time!"

Scraps blinked. She was staring at a ten-year-old dressed as a clown whose red putty nose was now veering dangerously to the left. Detectives are supposed to exude an authoritative air. Scraps could have said quite a lot at that precise moment, but instead she said nothing. Sometimes, if you can't say anything nice, it's best not to say anything at all.

"Gorgeous is always hanging around Cecily, so you can watch him and tell me if he says or does anything that might be a bit strange. Oh! And don't forget to think wonkily, because sometimes that helps!"

"All right," said Scraps with a small nod. "I'll do my best."

"SCRAAAAAAAAAAAAAAAPS!" came another scream from the next room.

"I'd better go. And, Wilma . . ." Scraps paused in the doorway. "Be careful."

Wilma followed Scraps to the door and gave her a silent thumbs-up as she disappeared into Cecily Lovely's dressing room. She took a deep breath. Going undercover was extremely thrilling, and with her new Man on the Inside she was confident that the case would be within solving distance before she knew it. She only wished she could see Mr. Goodman and tell him about all her adventures without him. But it would have to wait. She turned to go back into her dressing room and yelped. Standing in front of her was the old cleaner, huddled over his broom.

"A theatre is full of ears and tongues," he hissed from under his beard. "Now then. Rubbish! Any rubbish? Rubbish tells you all you need to know!" And off he went, having collected the discarded greasepaint-remover pots from her room.

Wilma pursed her lips. There was something about that old man she didn't like. But she had far more important things to think about. Like performing in the show that night. And keeping the rest of the cast alive. And catching a killer. So not much, then.

20

"Righto," said Inspector Lemone, closing his eyes and grimacing. "I think I've got it . . . No . . . no, I haven't. You're going to have to explain it to me again."

Penbert shoved her glasses to the top of her nose and tried for the tenth time. "So Wilma gave me a seaweed sample . . ."

"Yes, I remember that bit." The Inspector nodded, his eyes shut tight with concentration. "Where's Wilma? Thought she'd be here. Oh, never mind that. Seaweed. Right. Why was there seaweed again?"

"Because there was some seaweed in a bucket in Baron von Worms's office."

"Nice place. Bit cluttered. Costume in the shape of an owl. So far totally with you." Inspector Lemone nodded furiously.

Penbert rolled her eyes. "So I analyzed the seaweed and have discovered that, when certain conditions preside, it can become toxic."

"Errrr . . ."

"Because this seaweed," said Penbert, battling on, "has bobbles. And inside the bobbles is an enzyme . . ."

"Ooooooh," burbled Inspector Lemone.

"An enzyme," plowed on Penbert, "that is activated by phosphorous light."

"Phospho-what?" cried out Inspector Lemone.

"Phosphorous!" yelled Penbert in exasperation. "It's stuff that shines in the dark. When this particular seaweed comes into contact with this particular light, it becomes poisonous!"

"I can't see! Is there some sort of blinding light in my eyes?" yelled the Inspector, grabbing at the air in front of him. "Very hot! Confused! Sea-weed!"

"Calm down, Inspector!" boomed Dr. Kooks, taking the Inspector by the shoulders. "You're being blinded by science. It's only temporary. The feeling will pass in a few moments. Try to relax. I know Penbert can be a bit intense, but facts are facts and it's her job to tell you them."

"Here," suggested Penbert, pulling up a chair. "Sit down and I'll draw some non-threatening shapes on the blackboard instead."

"Yes, yes," gulped Inspector Lemone, dabbing at his eyes with his handkerchief. "Sorry, Kooks. It's all a little bit overwhelming."

"Don't worry," answered Dr. Kooks, giving his friend a firm pat on the shoulder. "We see this all the time. Although the reactions aren't usually quite as severe as yours. Still, never mind. Plan B, Penbert. Blackboard!"

Penbert was already standing, chalk in hand, at a small blackboard that she had wheeled over in front of the Inspector. Clearing her throat and in as soft a voice as she could muster, she began,

"So this shape is like a seaweed. And look," she added, drawing an upward curve, "it's smiling. But hang on! Here comes a naughty shape . . ."

"Looks like a squid," said the Inspector, pointing.

"Good man," said Dr. Kooks with another pat. "You can get through this."

"It's the phosphorus! And oh no!" said Penbert, her voice rising a little. "It's made the seaweed shape sad. And VERY dangerous! VERY, VERY dangerous!" Penbert, seizing the moment, quickly drew an enormous pair of fangs with some blood dripping from them on the seaweed, finished off the scene with a quick skull and crossbones, underlined it all with a flourish, and turned to face the Inspector. "Now do you get it?" she asked, panting slightly.

Inspector Lemone, whose face looked as if it had slipped sideways in the confusion, gulped and wiped his forehead. "I think . . ." he began slowly, "that I do. I do! I get it!"

"Oh, thank Cooper for that!" said Penbert, slumping over the blackboard.

"So that's the theory! Whoever is perpetrating these foul deeds is extremely clever. Now all we have to do is find the poison that's made from the seaweed. It's hidden in something!" shouted Dr. Kooks, thrusting a finger into the air. "And, not only that, but we need to discover who has access to phosphorous light and where it's coming from!"

"But how are we going to do that?" whimpered Inspector Lemone, biting his lip.

"By returning to the theatre, Inspector!" bellowed the forensic scientist triumphantly. "Goodman has gone! Dire times call for dire measures! Pack the bags, Penbert!" he continued, reaching for a large syringe. "We're going on a field trip!"

"Oh good," muttered Penbert weakly. Because after the day she'd just had, a field trip would be great. Just great.

21

The cry rang through the theatre, dreadful and despairing. "Oh no!" it sounded. "My mother! Help me! Someone help me!"

Lying on the floor of the laundry room was Mrs. Grumbletubs, looking as dead as a doornail, her mouth frothing with foam.

The killer had struck again.

Poor Geoffrey, who was in a terrible state, was led away by Malcolm Poppledore as the rest of the cast and crew gathered in the doorway. Wilma, who had heard the screams and come running, was straining to see through the crowd.

"Out of my way," yelled Barbu, waving his cane as he swept up behind them. "What's happened now?"

"It's Mrs. Grumbletubs," said Eric Ohio, shaking. "Dead! DEAD!"

"Yes, I can see that," snapped Barbu, bending down over her body. "What a terrible waste," he added with a small shake of his head. "No one paid to see her die."

"Hang on," chipped in Janty, who was peering over his master's shoulder. "What's that pinned to her apron?" He reached down and unhooked the attached note. It was made from cut-out letters, just like the other one Wilma had seen. "It's from the killer!" he announced, holding it out for everyone to see.

WILL YOU DIE ON STAGE TONIGHT?

A terrified gasp rippled through the assembled throng.

"Oh well," retorted Barbu, brightening. "That's

something, I suppose. Put another poster up, Janty! And if any of you DO die—make sure it's onstage! Be professional about it! Is that too much to ask?"

"You're a monster, Barbu D'Anvers!" heaved Cecily Lovely, gripping the door frame for support.

"Thanks!" replied Barbu. "I do my best. Janty! Tully! Let's go! We have an audience to cram in!"

"Hang on a minute!" wailed Eric Ohio, throwing his arms into the air. "Why are we even going on? What are we thinking? This is madness! MADNESS!"

Cecily shot the diminutive dummy a sharp glance. "Don't be ridiculous, Eric!" she wailed. "We are actors! There is an audience! The show MUST go on!"

"It's true," said Mrs. Wanderlip with a sigh, "it really must."

"Don't worry, Cecily," said Gorgeous Muldoon, stepping forward to put an arm around the stricken diva. "Nothing will happen to you. I will make sure of it."

255

Wilma's eyes widened and she gave Pickle a nudge. "Did you hear that?" she whispered. "He's going to make sure nothing happens to her! Well, of course he is! He's not going to bump off his girlfriend, is he? Maybe that's it! Maybe he's so insanely jealous he wants her all to himself? That's quite a good motive. I'd better write that down. *And* I bet he made that note as well. Maybe we can sneak around later. See if there are any scissors or glue in his dressing room."

Ducking into a dark corner in the corridor, Wilma got out her notebook and thought hard. Mrs. Grumbletubs's death seemed to throw some of her theories skyward. She wasn't listed on the playbill, nor was her death onstage, like the others. But she had seemed very agitated when she had spoken to her earlier. Mrs. Grumbletubs must have known something! And, somehow, the killer had gotten wind of it. Wilma felt a surge of regret. Perhaps she could have done something sooner and prevented this ghastly incident . . . And poor Geoffrey . . . he was an orphan now, like her.

"I think this," she whispered to Pickle as she scribbled, "is what my textbook refers to as a 'rubbing out of a witness.' Gorgeous Muldoon is getting desperate. We need to nail him down once and for all!"

"Excuse me, young lady," said someone approaching from up the corridor. "Could you tell me where the laundry room is, please?"

Wilma looked up. It was Inspector Lemone! Suppressing a small smile, she pointed into the doorway still packed with staring performers. "In there. Mrs. Grumbletubs has been killed. Looks like the same killer as before. There's foam and everything."

"Thank you," said the Inspector, stopping to mop his forehead. "Had to rush here straight from the lab. Quite a distance. Dr. Kooks, the body's in there by all accounts."

"Excuse us, thank you!" boomed the doctor, pushing through the small crowd, Penbert in tow.

Inspector Lemone was about to follow them in, but on seeing Pickle he stopped and frowned. "Funny-looking thing," he muttered, gesturing toward the trussed-up beagle. "What is he? Some sort of pig? Goat? Can't quite make it out."

Wilma, trying not to laugh so as not to blow her cover, shook her head. "No, he's a caaat."

"Cat, eh?" answered Inspector Lemone with some surprise. "Goodness! I know someone who'd like to give you a good chase! Ha-ha! By golly!"

Pickle stared blankly upward. Could Inspector Lemone *really* be that gullible? Yes. Yes, he really could.

"Anyway, best get on with this mucky business. Excuse me, 'scuse me, Inspector coming through!"

As he pushed his way through the gathered actors, Wilma squeezed into a small gap between Mrs. Wanderlip and the paper tearer, Countess Honey Piccio. Penbert was down on her knees examining the strange foam that was still bubbling from poor Mrs. Grumbletubs's mouth. "It's not the same," she said, frowning.

"And it has a different, very distinctive odor. With your permission, Dr. Kooks, I'd like to do a field analysis here rather than taking her back to the lab. I think the sooner we solve this problem, the better."

Dr. Kooks nodded. "I agree. Let's clear the area. Make the laundry room a makeshift lab. Inspector, see to it, if you please? We shall need everybody out, a table to work on, and a large pot of tea."

"Is it that phosphorous hoo-ha?" whispered Inspector Lemone, bending down to take a closer look.

"Phosphorous?" shouted the crazy old cleaner, lurking in the corner. "What's that got to do with anything?"

"Might be how the poison is activated," began Inspector Lemone. "In fact, we were on our way to find out where it might be coming from. I just checked the lights at front of stage. They're all gas lights. So it's not them. Then I heard the scream . . ." Penbert shot him a sharp glance. "Oh. Not supposed to say police business out loud," added Lemone, catching Penbert's glare. "Just pretend you didn't hear it. Right then, the lot of you, off you go. Let the scientists do their work! And don't panic! We'll have this solved in no time!"

Much to her annoyance, Wilma, with the others, was bundled away from the laundry room. "I need to find out more about the foss-fuss thing," she said quietly to Pickle. "What is it? How does it work? I think it might be time to tell the Inspector who we really are . . ."

But Pickle, squashed up against a tea crate, was shoving his nose upward. He'd seen something and wanted Wilma to see it too. Standing on tiptoe, Wilma strained to look. There he was! Gorgeous Muldoon! And he was heading into Cecily Lovely's dressing room!

"Okay," Wilma whispered. "We'll just see what he's up to, then we'll go and find Inspector Lemone." After all, Wilma reasoned, the show was about to start. Gorgeous could administer the poison at any moment!

Squeezing past everyone and then carefully

creeping closer, Wilma could hear the actress sobbing. No change there, of course, but underneath it rumbled the distinct deep tones of Gorgeous Muldoon. "But I thought that's what you wanted?" he was whispering. "To be the only person on the bill?"

Wilma poked Pickle hard in the ribs. This was a proper motive, make no mistake! Hearing someone approach behind her in the corridor, Wilma straightened and walked quickly past Cecily's open door. She looked in as she passed. Gorgeous was standing next to Cecily and in his hand . . . there was the bucket, with some seaweed still poking out of it! Wilma almost burst. Scooping up Pickle quickly, she swept back into their dressing room.

"He's bumping them all off to make Cecily a bigger star!" she panted. "Perhaps they're in it together! And did you see the bucket? Oh, Pickle! The net is tightening good and proper! Now all we have to do is see him administer the poison and we've got him! We have to tell Inspector Lemone immediately!"

Pickle wanted to agree but, at that precise moment, he was more concerned about the rear end of his tutu, which was causing him all manner of inconveniences. Still, at least he was suffering for his art. That was the main thing.

22

"Thank you," said Mrs. Grumbletubs, handing Inspector Lemone the empty teacup. "I'm feeling much better now. I don't know what happened. I was carrying my laundry basket in and there was someone in here. I don't know what they were doing and I couldn't see who it was because my basket was in the way. Next thing I know I was out cold."

"You obviously disturbed the killer," opined Inspector Lemone, who felt a sudden obligation to say something official. "They must have been unable to administer the poison, so they hit you on the head instead. Fiendish. You've had a lucky escape, Mrs. Grumbletubs!"

"I've patched up the bump on the back of your head," said Penbert with an organized sniff. "You were clearly struck from behind. And when you fell you knocked over this bottle of fabric softener, which must have dripped into your mouth. That's what caused the foaming. You can clean that up now," she added, gesturing to the old cleaner who was standing, mop in hand. "I no longer need to analyze it."

"I once dealt with a man killed by fabric softener," cut in Dr. Kooks, sensing an opportunity for an anecdote. "I did the autopsy. He had the softest internal organs I've ever seen. And his liver smelled of pinecones. Nasty business."

Everyone nodded in agreement. "Still," added Penbert with a stiff nod, "at least you're all right now, Mrs. Grumbletubs. No wonder everyone thought you were dead. You were out cold. And, what with the foam, I'm not surprised people jumped to conclusions. It's only to be expected. They're not professional scientists. Like I am."

"Ohhhh!" There came a small yell from the doorway. "B-b-but"—Wilma stumbled, pointing at the laundry mistress—"you're dead!"

"Not dead, thankfully. Just a bump to the head," explained Inspector Lemone, taking Wilma's arm and gently steering her back to the corridor. "Nothing to worry about."

"Inspector Lemone!" whispered Wilma. "It's me! Wilma! I'm undercover! And so is Pickle!" She pulled off Pickle's toast ears.

"Well, I never," replied the Inspector, plainly astonished. "I say—you were right about that seaweed, Wilma! Penbert says it's the source of the poison!"

"I knew it! Well, I've discovered something even more important!" Wilma hissed, grabbing Inspector Lemone by the forearm. "Gorgeous Muldoon is definitely the killer! I heard him telling Cecily that he wants to make her the only person on the bill AND he was standing with a bucket of seaweed!"

"Greasepaints!" shouted Malcolm Poppledore, coming up the corridor behind them.

"There you go. Fresh for tonight. Show starts in five minutes!"

Wilma took a tube and turned back to the Inspector. "If he's going to try to kill people tonight, then we have to move fast. I'm going to go on first and see if I can find any clues about how he's administering the poison. As soon as I see him make his move, we'll have him, Inspector!"

"Hang on, though, Wilma," cautioned Inspector Lemone, suddenly troubled. "This is a very dangerous fellow. I'm not sure you should go on at all!"

"But I'm not on the list! He's only killing people on the playbill! He hasn't killed Mrs. Grumbletubs and he only banged me on the head, remember! I'll be fine. We can catch him in the act and nobody else will get hurt!"

"Hmmm," thought the Inspector, still frowning. "I suppose you're right. But be careful. And don't let him come at you with a weird light. He's activating the poison with some sort of phosphorus. Still don't know where he's hiding the poison, though. So stay sharp. I'll finish up here with

Penbert and Kooks. You get yourself ready. I'll be in the wings, so if anything does happen, I'll be there."

"I've just got to reapply my greasepaint," Wilma enthused, giving the tube a little shake. "Oh! And you might want to ask Mrs. Grumbletubs why she was so scared when she was talking to me earlier. She told me she'd seen something. This is it, Inspector. I just know it! Mr. Goodman will be so pleased with us!"

Inspector Lemone watched Wilma as she ran off toward the stage. "I hope he is," he muttered under his breath, before turning back into the laundry room. "Now then, Mrs. Grumbletubs, apparently you saw something suspicious?"

"I s'pose I should have said something earlier, 'bout what I seen," Mrs. Grumbletubs confessed, her head hanging low. "But I was afraid for Geoffrey. It was my flashlight, you see. The one I use to spot the stubborn stains. And I saw the smoking."

"Smoking?" asked Penbert with a frown. "Where?"

"Off the stains," explained Mrs. Grumbletubs, handing Penbert a dirty collar. "But I only saw it when I used my flashlight."

"And where's the flashlight?" asked Inspector Lemone, looking around. "Sounds like important evidence!"

"It's gone," said Mrs. Grumbletubs, pointing to an empty hook.

"Well, there we have it," announced Inspector Lemone, flushed with achievement. "The killer must have come in here to steal your flashlight! You discovered the fiend in the act and the rest is history!"

Penbert took the collar and placed it under her microscope. There was a large flesh-colored smudge on it. "Look, Inspector," said Penbert, unusually excited. "Mrs. Grumbletubs is right. On the face of it, it would appear to be an ordinary dirty collar. The flashlight you were using must have contained a form of phosphorus. Look what happens to it when I switch on this phosphorescent light device that I made all on my own with no one helping me."

"Do get on with it, Penbert," rumbled Dr. Kooks, pacing.

Penbert lowered a small lever on her microscope and a strange blue light shone downward onto the collar. Everyone bent forward to watch. A heavy silence filled the room. Nothing.

"It's just a light. On a collar," said Inspector Lemone, a little puzzled.

"Wait!" cried Penbert.

Suddenly, a small, almost invisible vapor wafted up from the collar. "Good grief!" shouted Lemone, standing upright and clamping a hand to his nose. "It's the same smell as the poison!"

"That's because it IS the poison!" yelled Penbert triumphantly. "The poison when activated emits a vapor that when inhaled is deadly! We have discovered HOW it's being administered! The phosphorous light reacts with the poison, creating a vapor that is easily inhaled into the lungs, which then creates the foam that causes the choking. The poison is coming from the smudge. The poison, Inspector, is in the GREASEPAINT!"

"Well, well," said the befuddled Inspector,

shaking his head. "In the greasepaint? What a fiendishly clever thing to do. In the greasepaint, eh? Pfffft. Greasepaint. Well, I never. Hang on a minute . . ." he added, panic setting in. "Greasepaint? Oh no! Wilma!"

Oh yes. Wilma. Not another close scrape with death? Here we go again . . .

23

The thunder of applause had been deafening. The auditorium, as Wilma and Pickle took the stage, was packed to the rafters. Everyone had come to see if more people would die. Wilma looked out and gulped. Performing their dance routine in front of so many people was extremely daunting, but there was no turning back now. She looked down at Pickle. His back leg was shaking uncontrollably. Not only that, but the involuntary smells were back. "Just pretend they're rows of cabbages," whispered Wilma, placing a reassuring hand on his head.

"Or they're sitting in nothing but their underpants."

Wilma gestured to the conductor in the orchestra pit and the music for their routine began to swell. "There he is!" she said as she struck her first pose. "Gorgeous Muldoon! In the wings! Keep your eyes peeled, Pickle!"

Pickle, who was shimmying his rear end with considerable vigor, shot a quick look sideways at Gorgeous, lurking in the darkness. There was no doubt about it—menace most foul was afoot.

"He's just standing there!" hissed Wilma from the side of her mouth as she kneeled down and clicked her fingers. "He's got something in his hand! Is it the foss-fuss light? Maybe we shouldn't wait for him to make a move? Maybe," she panted as Pickle jumped up onto her shoulders, "we should confront him now? Try and arrest him or something? Oh, I wish Mr. Goodman was here!" But Pickle couldn't think about that at this particular moment. He had a tricky yet dazzling dance move to pull off.

Behind Gorgeous in the wings, the crazy cleaner

suddenly appeared from nowhere. Wilma was trying to watch, but they'd reached the point in their routine where they had to do synchronized neck rolls. As they spun to the left, Wilma could see the crazy cleaner creeping up behind Gorgeous. She frowned. She turned to the front. Frustration coursed through her! All she wanted to do was bring Gorgeous Muldoon to justice once and for all! Their heads snapped upward and as Wilma leaped up and stepped sideways to take position for the end of their act, she snuck a quick peek back toward the wings once more. Something had happened! Gorgeous was on the floor and standing over him was the crazy cleaner! What was going on?

Wilma could now see Inspector Lemone, Penbert, and Dr. Kooks in the opposite wing. The Inspector was shouting and gesturing wildly at her, but, with the music reaching its crescendo, she couldn't make out what he was saying. She looked back toward Gorgeous, who was on his feet again and seemed to be holding back the cleaner, who, for some reason, was trying to get onto the stage.

But just then the music swelled for the big end to their routine. Wilma didn't know what to do. Should she drop the act and rush over to the wings to investigate further, knowing that if she did the game would be up? Or should she see the show through? Mrs. Speckle had been quite clear—the show must ALWAYS go on. Wilma would have to finish!

They kicked, turned, and kicked again, the main lights dimmed, and a narrow, piercing spotlight fell on Wilma's face. But something wasn't right. A strange sensation crept over her. A stabbing, scratchy numbness filled the back of her throat. She was struggling to breathe! She had to make it to the end of the routine! Shimmy! Shimmy! Throat getting tighter! Jazz hands! As she raised her arms to shake them, the theatre began to swirl. Pickle became a blur and the intense light was blinding!

"The p-p-poison . . ." she gasped, clutching at her throat as her knees buckled and the world went black.

Suddenly, from nowhere, someone had scooped

her into his arms. She could feel a wet cloth on her face wiping ferociously and rapidly. Water was being poured into her mouth and, as if being yelled at through a thick fog, she could hear a voice telling her to gargle and spit. Somewhere, through the molasses of confusion she could hear Inspector Lemone shouting, "It's the greasepaint! The greasepaint!" but all she could do was drift in and out of consciousness.

After a while, Wilma felt her breathing begin to regulate, the terrible scratching in her throat eased, and, burping one large unpleasant-smelling bubble from her mouth, she opened her eyes. She flinched. She was lying in the arms of the crazy old cleaner!

"Who *are* you?" she whispered, gazing up at him.

Throwing the greasepaint-covered towel to the floor, the man stood to his full height and with an impressive flourish pulled off his hat and beard. "It's me, Wilma," he said in as serious a tone as he could muster. "Theodore P. Goodman! I'm back!"

Please feel free to cheer.

"Gather everybody to the stage!" Theodore announced, his deep voice resounding around the auditorium. "I have been operating undercover as a theatre cleaner so that I could continue my investigation into these murders in secret. In my disguise I was able to hear and see things that might have gone unnoticed. But my work is now done. This case is about to be solved once and for all!"

An air of shocked expectancy bristled from the front of the stalls to the back of the upper circle. Some of the audience were on their feet and, everywhere, urgent mutterings filled the theatre. Theodore, handing Wilma over to Penbert, turned to face the gathering performers and backstage staff. He was still dressed in his cleaner's disguise, but his uncovered golden hair and magnificent caramel-colored mustache glistened in the footlights. He had returned in triumph.

Inspector Lemone, who had been completely at sea since the disappearance of his friend and colleague, was experiencing a flush of such intense relief that all he could do was buy two boxes of corn crumbles from a passing usher and consume them immediately.

"What is the meaning of this?" yelled Barbu D'Anvers, bustling onto the stage. "Why has the show stopped? I demand that it continue!"

"Mr. Goodman is claiming to have solved the case," answered Baron von Worms sharply. "You'll have to wait until he's finished!"

"Poppycock!" blared the diminutive villain. "People have paid to see a grisly show! Not a boring washed-up detective drone on!"

"Let Mr. Goodman speak!" shouted a voice from the back of the stalls.

"Yes!" shouted another from the dress circle. "I want to know who did it!"

Barbu's eyes narrowed. If there's one thing a short man hates, it's being contradicted. His hands tightened into fists. Someone, somewhere, was about to feel his wrath, but, annoyingly, there were too many audience members to choose from. And quite a lot of them were bigger than him. Not that that meant he was small. Oh no. Still, he was a terrible man and he had standards to keep up. So he turned and hit Tully on the forehead with his cane instead.

"Ow! What was that for?" moaned the long-suffering henchman, rubbing his head.

Janty stared at Wilma, still in her clown's outfit. "You were Maude Muddle?" he asked, frowning. "I can't believe you fooled me . . . You were really good."

Wilma nodded and burped another foul-smelling belch.

"If everyone is gathered," interjected Theodore, looking serious and noble, "then I shall begin."

The undercurrent of mumbles from the audience fell silent.

Theodore took center stage. You could have heard a pin drop. "This case began with a death by poisoning. A poison that caused the victims to, in effect, be strangled from the inside out. But we didn't know where the poison was coming from or how it was being administered. At first, we thought it was someone with a grudge against the mind reader Sabbatica, but when the Great Sylvester also fell victim to the poison's ghastly grip, it was clear that a more complicated intention was afoot. Money seemed to be the primary motive! An insurance policy came to light," continued the great detective, "one that guaranteed Baron von Worms a massive payout in the event of unnatural deaths."

"I knew it was him!" rattled Eric Ohio, his wooden head shooting upward. "NEVER trust the management!"

"Shhh, Eric," soothed Mrs. Wanderlip, pulling down his flapping arm as everyone turned to look at the Baron, letting slip a weak smile.

"But what if someone else had access to the Baron's office?" opined the great detective, holding a finger in the air. "They could have seen the insurance policy. And the fact that someone sent it quite deliberately to Inspector Lemone suggested that the Baron was being set up. The Baron was not the killer."

"Yes!" shouted the Baron, punching the air.

"In fact, the killer was quite keen to send me several red herrings," continued Theodore. "Because not only did we receive the insurance policy pointing a finger at the Baron, but we were also sent a sinister letter made from cut-up letters. It was as if the killer enjoyed the terror, the drama of a game of deadly anticipation. And, just today, another collage letter was found pinned to the unconscious body of Mrs. Grumbletubs. But every letter leaves a trail of clues, and that was the killer's mistake. Because during my time here, undercover as a cleaner, I made it my business to take note of everyone's rubbish."

"Oh!" gasped Wilma, suddenly remembering. "That's what you meant when you told me that rubbish tells you everything you need to know!"

"Correct! And I can now reveal that I found this . . ." Theodore reached into the inside pocket of his waistcoat and pulled out a large, crumpled piece of paper. As he unfolded it, a small gasp rang out through the auditorium. "It's the front page of yesterday's *Early Worm* and, as you can see, many of the letters have been cut out!"

"But where did you find it, Mr. Goodman?" called out Wilma, before burping another yellow bubble.

"I found it in the wastepaper basket of . . . Countess Honey Piccio!"

"Of course it was her!" screamed Eric, flinging an arm in her direction. "She's the paper tearer! She has access to loads of paper! How could we have been so blind!"

Now everyone turned to stare at the Countess.

"Bit like watching tennis," mumbled Inspector Lemone, rubbing his neck.

"I resent the implication!" cried the Countess,

clasping her hands. "I often have torn paper in my wastepaper basket. That doesn't prove anything!"

"Indeed," Theodore agreed ambiguously, much to everyone's further confusion. "And so we come back to the poison. Penbert had some results and was able to reveal that the putrid substance had come from a plant."

"A plant?" yelled Eric Ohio in a frenzy. "Geoffrey's crazy about plants! It was him! It was Geoffrey Grumbletubs! No wonder he didn't kill his mother!"

Everyone turned to stare at the teenager. Startled at the attention, he flushed bright red. "Shut up, Eric!" he complained. "Of course it wasn't me! Don't be ridiculous!"

"It was the seaweed!" burped Wilma, pulling herself off the stage floor. "I saw it in the bucket! I went to fetch some from Filthy Cove!"

"Filthy Cove?" shouted out Eric Ohio, his wooden head spinning sideways. "Then it really *is* Countess Honey Piccio! She's got a small bathing hut there. It *was* her! I knew it!"

"Disgraceful!" objected the Countess, flushed with indignity. "It certainly was not me!"

"But when I got there, someone was already there collecting seaweed!" added Wilma, her eyes widening. "And when they realized they were about to be caught red-handed they ran off, leaving a wooden finger behind them!"

"A wooden finger!" screamed Eric Ohio. "I knew it! It was Eric Ohio! The ventriloquist's dummy!"

"No, Eric," chided Mrs. Wanderlip, shaking her head. "That's you. You can't accuse yourself."

"Oh yes," mumbled the dummy, his head sinking into his chest.

"The wooden finger was significant," said Theodore, reaching for the Clue Bag in his waistcoat pocket and holding it out for everyone to see. "But this finger Wilma found did not belong to Eric Ohio!"

"See! See!" yelled the dummy, confident once more. "I knew it wasn't me!"

"But he's missing a finger, Mr. Goodman!" cried out Geoffrey, eager to get back at Eric. "It must be his!"

"No!" interjected Wilma, realizing what Theodore was getting at. "Look at the finger in Mr. Goodman's bag. It's a different color from the rest of Eric's hand. It's a different sort of wood. Eric lost his finger because the killer crept into his dressing room and stole his finger to make it look like he'd lost it at Filthy Cove! But that must mean there's someone else with a wooden finger? Am I right, Mr. Goodman? Is that what you meant when you said it was all change? You know, when you were a cleaner?"

"Precisely so, Wilma," said Theodore, nodding. "Yet again, it seemed to be another false trail. But the seaweed was the key to the unraveling of this miserable mystery. People were dying onstage with no one near them. Not only that, but how was the poison being administered? Penbert discovered that the deadly enzyme was being hidden in the actors' greasepaint and that it was activated by phosphorescent light. As soon as the intended victims stepped onstage, they were doomed. Without knowing it, they were poisoning themselves!"

"It's actually a fascinating biological compound," said Penbert, stepping forward and clearing her throat for a full analysis. "The chlorophyll in the—"

"Not now, Penbert," said Dr. Kooks, pulling her back.

"Hang on!" squawked Eric Ohio, his wooden head now rotating very quickly. "In the greasepaints? But there's only one person in charge of the greasepaints! Malcolm Poppledore! It was him! I knew it!"

"Malcolm Poppledore was in charge of the greasepaints, yes," answered Theodore patiently. "But he merely distributed the fresh deliveries. He was no more aware of what he was handing out than the poor unfortunates who applied it for the last time. The killer was not Malcolm Poppledore!"

"Oh, thank goodness," heaved Malcolm, who had gone a bit sweaty.

"But it was under the stage where the greasepaints are mixed each day that the mystery would unravel further. My apprentice was struck on the back of the head after she chanced upon the killer, just as Mrs. Grumbletubs did when she stumbled into the laundry at the precise moment that the fiend was stealing her phosphorescent flashlight—a vital clue that would reveal how the poison was being activated."

"This is the foss-fuss bit, Pickle," explained Wilma, putting her arm around her beagle. "Try to keep up."

"Phosphorus," explained Theodore, turning to look at his apprentice. "Not foss-fuss. And this isn't that bit quite yet. I need to deal with the bumps on the head first, Wilma. Remember, it's important for detectives to be methodical in their final summing up. You can look that up in your textbook later."

Everyone turned and looked at Wilma and shook their heads and tutted.

Wilma mustered a weak smile. "Sorry," she mouthed.

And Theodore carried on. "So my assistant was bumped on the head. The reason? She had disturbed the killer as the deadly seaweed was being mixed into the greasepaints. Not only that, but Wilma was about to find the clue that would prove most decisive in solving this case—an old playbill for this theatre on which the names of the victims so far were crossed off. So who was it? And what was the strange creaking that Wilma heard just before she was hit on the head? It was the sound of a pair of brand-new leather shoes. And there is only one person here who has recently been complaining of uncomfortable new shoes!"

"Gorgeous Muldoon!" cried out Wilma, fit to burst, pointing toward the grumpy comedian still sitting on the floor. "It was him! He was the one! He's in love with Cecily and wanted her to be the only person on the bill, Mr. Goodman! I even saw him with a bucket of seaweed!"

"I knew it was him!" shouted Eric Ohio, his arms flying upward.

"What?" shouted Gorgeous, struggling to his feet. "I do have new shoes, but what does that have to do with anything? And the bucket was full of seawater! To soak my blistered feet in! Since when has that been a crime?"

Wilma shook her head. "But . . ."

"Mr. Muldoon's shoes did creak, Wilma, you are entirely correct," interjected Theodore, at which Wilma shot Gorgeous a smug glance. "But it was not Mr. Muldoon who was wearing them at the time of your attack."

Wilma did a double take. "But," she began, "if he wasn't wearing them, then who was?"

"I found those shoes"—he paused dramatically to point—"in the dressing room of Cecily Lovely!"

A ripple of shock passed through the audience. So great was the surprise that several gentlemen fainted and one woman near the front punched another woman in a flouncy hat.

Cecily shook her head a little and blinked. "D-don't be ridiculous," she stuttered. "I can't even walk if I'm not in a sufficient heel."

"Precisely so," added Theodore, "so why would a lady require a gentleman's shoes?"

"Gentleman's shoes?" blustered Cecily, fanning herself suddenly. "I never saw . . . I mean . . . sometimes I like to throw things . . . Perhaps they were there for that . . . Gorgeous! Help me!"

"I know why the shoes were there," said Gorgeous, stepping forward to take Cecily in his arms. "I left them there because I wanted them polished and stretched. Cecily had nothing to do with it. They were there to be dealt with by her dresser. Nothing improper."

"And so," Theodore intoned, "we return to the most crucial and decisive clue of all, the playbill. Two years ago, all of you here present were already at the Valiant Vaudeville Theatre!"

"D'Anvers Vau-Devil!" shouted Barbu in protest. "It's got a new name! NEW name!"

But Theodore powered on. "One name was missing from this playbill, torn from the bottom of the page."

"You have to look for what's not there!" shouted Wilma, recalling Theodore's first cryptic clue. "You wanted me to find out about the missing name on the playbill!"

"A name that the killer wanted to remain forgotten." Theodore nodded. "Mysterious Mezmo, specializing, I found out from a theatrical review of that night's show that I found in the *Early Worm* archives, in a strange light show. A light show that dealt with phosphorescence."

"Thank Cooper for critics!" exclaimed Cecily. "I've always loved them!"

"Ooh," whispered Wilma, giving Pickle a nudge. "Now it's the foss . . . I mean, phosphorous bit."

"But Mezmo was masked, nobody saw the illusionist's face, and, what was more, every single illusion went wrong. There was an explosion, during which Mezmo lost a finger. A finger that I can only presume was replaced with a wooden one later. The performer was booed offstage, not just by the audience but by all of you here. Mezmo, humiliated, disappeared. But the humiliation felt that night cut a wound so deep that the first seeds of a desire for revenge were sown."

"I love this bit, but I can't bear the tension!" cried out Inspector Lemone, clutching his hands together.

"Mysterious Mezmo was never seen again," carried on Theodore as everyone stood rapt. "But the person behind the mask returned and that person is here now."

Wilma glanced frantically about the assembled cast and crew. Who could it be?

"Revenge was the motive!" declared Theodore dramatically. "Mezmo wanted to be in the bright lights! But was shunned and banned from doing so! Mezmo had died onstage! And was determined that everyone else at the Valiant would do the same—literally!"

"But who is it?" screamed Eric, unable to bear it any longer. "WHO?"

"Who had access to all these other people's rooms?" Theodore cried with passion. "Who was trusted enough by the Baron to be allowed into his office? To help Malcolm with the greasepaints? To help Gorgeous with his shoes? Who was it who operated the single light in the theatre that emitted a phosphorescence, thus activating the poison?" Theodore suddenly and without warning ran to the front of the stage, picked up one of the footlights, and, turning to face the audience, he swung it upward toward the scaffolding, where he pointed the beam straight into a squinting face above them all. "It was you! The person who was everyone's dogsbody! It was your job to clean out Countess Honey Piccio's trash can, you who tidied the Baron's office, you who wore Gorgeous Muldoon's shoes to stretch them out, you who prepared Cecily Lovely's plant-based potions, and you who operated the deadly spotlight! It was you, Scraps! You were Mysterious Mezmo and you are the killer!"

"Scraps!" gasped Wilma, grabbing on to Pickle with the shock. "It can't be!"

"Now, I didn't know that!" mumbled Eric Ohio, shaking his head.

Yes. It was Scraps. Of course it was. It's ALWAYS the quiet ones who are the worst. Everyone knows THAT.

25

Everyone stared up at the scrawny, scruffy
girl being held by the arms by a man in a
smart uniform. "Bring her down, Captain Brock!"
shouted Theodore at his colleague of old.

Captain Brock was the head of the island's
2nd Hawks Brigade. Whenever anything needed
watching very carefully, he was your man. He
also excelled at capturing and restraining, which
was why Theodore, who knew his nuts and bolts,
had called him in for the case's big ending.

Wilma looked down at Pickle. He was just
as surprised as she was. The killer was Scraps!

Wilma felt a sharp pang of sadness and regret. Scraps had been her friend. She had tried to help her. She'd even asked Scraps to be her Man on the Inside. If Wilma wanted to be a detective, she was going to have to do better than this.

Walking over to her mentor, she tugged at his trouser leg. "I could have sworn it was Gorgeous Muldoon, Mr. Goodman," she said, looking up at him. "Because he was always so weird and miserable."

"He's a comedian, Wilma," explained Theodore, sticking his thumbs into his waistcoat pockets. "They're always weird and miserable. And don't be too hard on yourself, Wilma. I know you were fond of Scraps. But villains often mask their true identities. You had all the right clues. You just let them go off in the wrong direction."

Scraps was led onto the stage by Captain Brock, her head hanging low. "This is an outrage," she muttered, shooting a sharp upward glance in the great detective's direction. "You've got nothing on me. Of course I'm allowed to go everywhere! I work here! I'm not Mezmo!"

"He's got the wrong man!" yelled Eric, panicking. "I mean woman! The killer's still on the loose!"

"There were two final things that led me to Scraps," answered Theodore, ignoring Eric's outburst. "First, I remembered that all of Cecily's facial treatments were uniquely prepared."

"I have very sensitive skin," Cecily announced self-importantly.

"You, Scraps, were making all her ointments using plants from lavender . . . to seaweed. Only you had the knowledge required to make the poisonous greasepaints. That's why the bucket with seawater and seaweed was in the Baron's office and then Cecily's dressing room, where Gorgeous saw it and thought he would use it for his blisters."

"That's right!" chipped in the grumpy comedian. "I did!"

"Second, there is the matter of the wooden finger that was found at Filthy Cove. Well done, Wilma. Your find has proved decisive. You were right. Someone other than Eric Ohio did have a wooden finger. Someone who never wanted their hands to be seen . . ."

"Scraps always wears gloves!" Wilma burst out. "She told me it was because she was allergic to boot polish and greasepaint!"

"Well," said Theodore, nodding, "it was very important that she didn't come into contact with the poisonous greasepaint. Especially as she was operating the phosphorescent light. But the gloves were mainly to hide the one thing that would have revealed her true identity. Captain Brock! Remove the gloves, if you please!"

"Certainly will!" barked Captain Brock, reaching for Scraps's hands. "Well, well!" he exclaimed, pulling the gloves off. "There it is! Bold as brass! A wooden finger on the right hand!"

"That's mine!" wailed Eric Ohio, arms flailing. "She's got my finger!"

Wilma, who was still very shocked, stepped forward, serious and somber. "You were my friend, Scraps. I know there is good in you somewhere. But what you've done is terrible. Why did you do it?"

Scraps, who had always seemed so quiet and shy, slowly raised her head to glare at them all fiercely. "My life was ruined that night! All I ever dreamed of was being onstage! And you all destroyed me. Especially you, Cecily! I swore that I would have my revenge! One by one I was going to kill you all! You would all die onstage! Just like I did! It took me a while to work out how I could do it, but I knew a deadly greasepaint was the perfect answer. None of you would suspect a thing! The greasepaint was quite safe until the poison was activated! The poison was phospho-sensitive. All I had to do was replace the theatre's old spotlight with my specially designed one and the poison would be triggered! Your lives were in my hands! My only regret is that I chose to kill you last of all, Cecily! You were to be my final victim. I wanted you to watch everyone around you fall one by one so that you would be half crazy with anxiety. I knew you would never leave the theatre. Your ego would never allow it!"

"You were going to kill me?" yelled Cecily,

appalled. "ME? How dare you! Well, I hope you're not expecting a reference!"

"Thankfully we have stopped you before you could complete your grim task," said Theodore sadly. "Revenge consumed you. You lost sight of the good, decent girl you once were. But you have committed terrible crimes, and for that you must be punished. Inspector Lemone, help Captain Brock take her away."

Wilma stood with Mr. Goodman watching Scraps being led to the steps down from the stage. It was always a somber moment to see someone being brought to justice, but there was satisfaction that another case had been successfully solved. Given that Wilma had thought of Scraps as her friend, the success was particularly bittersweet and she experienced a sadness that someone's life could have been so altered that she was driven to unspeakable deeds.

"Oh, and, Cecily," Scraps said, turning just as she was about to descend, "you know that pampas-grass ointment that I've been putting on your face for the last year?"

"The one that rejuvenates AND lifts?" replied Cecily. "Yes. What about it?"

"Actually, it's an ageing cream," snapped Scraps triumphantly. "It GIVES you wrinkles."

"Oh . . . oh . . . OHHHHHHHHHHHH!" screamed Cecily before fainting dead away.

"Someone pick her up," groaned Barbu, who had had just about enough of all this nonsense. Turning to the audience, he held his hands out. "Don't worry! The killer may have been caught, but I can guarantee that standards at the Vau-DEVIL will not slip!"

"Excuse me," said a small, neatly presented woman approaching the stage from the back of the auditorium. She had flame-red hair scraped into a tight ponytail and a distinctive lumpy mole on her left cheek. "Are you Barbu D'Anvers?"

"Yes," replied Barbu dismissively. "But I'm not doing autographs now. Speak to my assistant, Janty. He'll sort you out."

"I'm afraid you've misunderstood," answered the woman, pulling out a clipboard and tapping it with a perfectly sharpened pencil. "My name is Swinnerton. I'm the Health and Safety Officer for all public buildings on Cooper. And it's come to my attention that four people have been killed here while at work."

"Yes, so?" snapped Barbu, stepping to the edge of the stage and sneering down at her.

"Then I am afraid that under Regulation four-five-seven-D subsection sixty-three, you, as the manager of this theatre, are financially liable. As such, you are required to pay the following sum of money." She took a small slip of paper and handed it up to Barbu. He grabbed it and snorted.

"This is a joke, yes?" he spluttered. "Three hundred thousand and ninety-four ginorma-grogs? Don't be ridiculous. That's more than I've taken at the theatre. That's more money than I could possibly EVER make. If I had to give you that, I'd be ruined! As if! Tully! Make her go away!"

"Oh, I already have the money," retorted Officer Swinnerton with a short sniff. "I seized it from your accounts an hour ago. I'm merely here as a courtesy to tell you I've done it. Here's a copy of your bank account statement," she added, handing up a second piece of paper.

Barbu took it, stared, then blinked. "My bank account is empty?" he whispered. "EMPTY? After being stuck in this flea pit for a week? Tully! Do something! Punch someone! Break something! Janty! Destroy her! Quickly! I have nothing in my bank account! NOTHING!"

"And here," continued Officer Swinnerton, ignoring Barbu completely, "is a note of *my* fee. I should draw your attention to the extra grogs at the bottom. That's because I was called out on my day off. I will take cash. If it's easier."

Barbu was so shell-shocked, he looked as if he'd been dropped on his head. "You want me to PAY you for taking all my money?" he screamed, bending down to stare at her, wild-eyed.

"Yes please, Mr. D'Anvers," replied Officer Swinnerton calmly. "If you don't have cash, which clearly you don't, then we can always go to your home and I can seize property to the value of the debt. As I say, whatever is easiest."

Barbu screwed his lips into a tight ball. His face

had turned a deep crimson and he looked as if he was about to explode. "SEIZE my property?" he hissed.

"Well, to be honest," continued the woman with marked efficiency, "we have already. I just thought I'd stagger the bad news. So, in a nutshell, we've cleared out your bank account and we have seized all your property at Rascal Rock. Here's a bankruptcy form, which you may want to fill in. Obviously we were concerned that you are now homeless, so we've arranged for the three of you to be put up."

"And where might that be?" shouted Barbu.

"The only place on the island that had a cheap spare room, Mr. D'Anvers," replied Officer Swinnerton, fixing the villain with a steely glare. "At the Institute for Woeful Children."

Wilma, who, like everyone else in the theatre, had been watching this small drama unfold with interest, clamped a hand to her mouth. She could barely believe it.

"Oh, Pickle," she whispered, "I wouldn't wish that on my worst enemy." Stepping forward, she put her hand on Janty's forearm. "I lived at the Institute for Woeful Children for ten years," she said softly. "If you ever need any help—"

But Janty pulled his arm away from her. "I'll never need your help, Tenderfoot! Never!"

Barbu, on hearing this calamitous news, went a little stiff, burbled something incomprehensible, and collapsed backward into Tully's arms.

In the silence that followed, a voice rang out from the dress circle. "Well done, Goodman!" The sentiment was soon being echoed around the auditorium until applause filled the air, peppered with whistles and whoops and, onstage, Wilma turned to see the surviving cast and crew clapping too. Not used to the frivolities of show business, Theodore acknowledged the approval with nothing more than a small dignified nod, and then, tucking his magnifying glass into his waistcoat pocket, he descended from the stage and started up the center aisle toward the back of the theatre. And as he walked, everyone to his left and right rose to their feet. "Stand up," Wilma heard one man say to his son. "Mr. Goodman is passing."

And as Wilma looked around her, she understood that while there will always be people who brag and boast, there are also people like Mr. Goodman, who do great deeds quietly, and that it is they who deserve the loudest honors.

Hooray. Hooray. Hooray!

26

With the case done and dusted, things were getting back to normal at Clarissa Cottage. Mrs. Speckle was baking a fresh batch of corn crumbles, Inspector Lemone and Theodore were enjoying an afternoon game of Lantha, and Wilma and Pickle had been chasing each other around the garden, taking care not to crash into any of Mr. Goodman's roses.

It had been an exciting few weeks. Not only had Wilma been enrolled as an apprentice, but she had also learned a valuable lesson. Being a detective was far more complicated than it looked and just because Mr. Goodman made it seem easy didn't mean that she could just jump in at the deep end and hope for the best. Wilma would have to learn patience and stealth. This was how Mr. Goodman had solved the case, not by clattering about like a spinning top. Still, she had managed to think wonkily and that, at least, was a step in the right direction.

With this in mind, Wilma was now able to turn her attentions back to her own mysterious family investigations. A note from Penbert had revealed that the scrap of material she had sent for analysis was a piece of butcher's muslin. The foul, smelly stain was old pig's blood and the two crossed bones had been firmly identified as lamb chops. Perhaps she had been left at the Institute by a butcher? Or a farmer?

But as for the letters, Wilma was still all at sea. Somehow, she had to find out who had written them and where that person was. "It's impossible, Mr. Goodman," she said, shaking her head as she handed Theodore two of the letters. "The name on the bottom of the money ones is illegible. And there's no address. And this one, in the different handwriting, is a total mystery."

Theodore, who had just captured two of Inspector Lemone's Lantha pieces at once, leaned back into his armchair and took the letters. "On the contrary," he replied, briefly examining the notes. "Let's look at the one in the different handwriting. This letter is full of clues. A handwritten note is a unique calling card, as telling as a fingerprint or a limp. First, there's the paper it is written on. This writing paper is handmade. Look at the uneven edges. This tells me that the writer may be an artistic type or a free-thinker. The ink is thickly lain. You're looking for a pen with a fat nib. And the handwriting is a little erratic. This was written by someone in a hurry. Not only that, but look at the end of each sentence. Every single one has a small smudge at the tail end. Whoever wrote this note is probably wearing a ring on the little finger of their writing hand. All of these things, Wilma, are clues. Clues right in front of your eyes."

Wilma was astonished. "It's like some sort

of magic trick!" she said, face beaming. "Now you've pointed those things out, they seem obvious. I guess it's just another wonky way of thinking, isn't it, Mr. Goodman?"

"A little bit, yes," agreed the great detective with a nod. "Being a detective is all about using your eyes and ears, Wilma. And playing sharp."

"Playing pretty sharp at Lantha today, Goodman!" mumbled Inspector Lemone, who had had to take his two pieces back to the start. "Almost had them off the board then."

Theodore reached for his pipe. "A fortunate roll of the dice, Inspector," he said, getting out his rosemary tobacco. "What's our game tally now?"

Inspector Lemone pulled out his notebook and flicked to the back page. "Goodman versus Lemone," he read out, "Clarissa Cottage Championships. Wins. Goodman, three hundred fifty-eight. Lemone, zero. Although there was that time when I almost won. Perhaps I could add that?"

"Perhaps," said Theodore with a small smile. "Ahh! Mrs. Speckle!" he added as the door to his study swung open. "Peppermint tea!"

"And corn crumbles!" added the Inspector, jumping to his feet.

"Letter for Miss Wilma," muttered the ever grumpy housekeeper, laying the tea tray down on the study table. "Academy crest on it. Probably something official. And a review of Maude Muddle and her Amazing Cat Pizzazz in the *Early Worm,*" she added with a small wink.

"Really?" enthused Wilma, jumping over to the tea tray. "I've never had a review before. Oh wait. That's not true. I was in a play once when I was at the Institute for Woeful Children. My character was called Smelly Socks Bear. I was a bear. With smelly socks. Who also liked eating smelly socks. Madam Skratch said I was unconvincing." Wilma picked up the paper and flicked through to the Arts pages. "Here it is! Oh, Pickle! Listen to this!"

Maude Muddle and her Amazing Cat Pizzazz cut a brand-new dash at the Von Worms (formerly D'Anvers) Vaudeville Theatre last night. With their sassy moves and tight shimmies, this exciting new duo sparkled up a stage that, in recent times,

has been a little grisly and gloomy. The middle section, in which Pizzazz climbs atop Muddle, was a clever allegory of the eternal power struggle between man and cat, and although the rest of the piece lacked emotional depth or intelligence, their enthusiasm was certainly infectious. And Pizzazz looked great in his tutu.

Wilma looked up. "I can't quite work out whether that's a good review or a bad one," she said, a little confused. "And I have no idea what an allegory is. I just got Pickle to stand on my shoulders. I wasn't trying to be clever."

"Don't worry," explained Mrs. Speckle. "Critics always make stuff up to try to look brainy."

"Sparkled up the stage, eh?" commented Inspector Lemone, giving Pickle an encouraging pat. Pickle tried to look blasé, but was secretly delighted. Mostly because they'd said he looked good in his tutu.

"What does the letter from the Academy say, Wilma?" asked Theodore, taking a puff on his pipe.

"It's a report card," said Wilma, opening the

envelope and peering in. "Oh. It hasn't got anything on it. I think Miss Lambard must have forgotten to fill it out. She was quite busy when I last saw her. Perhaps I should go to the Academy this afternoon. I need to hand in my first homework on the Case of the Missing Relative in any event. Especially now you've given me so many letter clues."

"And you can tell her about the Case of the Putrid Poison too," chipped in Inspector Lemone, who was quite eager to say anything at that precise moment just so Mrs. Speckle would look at him.

"Yes!" agreed Wilma with a determined nod. "I might get extra credit for working on a proper case and collecting some proper clues of my own. Even if I did get the wrong end of the stick."

The walk to the Academy of Detection and Espionage was a short one. The sun was shining, the famous Cooper poppies were in bloom, and Wilma's head was full of scrawled notes and butcher's blood and what she should try next.

"I'll show Miss Lambard all the letters I've found," explained the plucky ten-year-old to her loyal beagle as they made their way through the secret entrance behind the statue of Anthony Amber. "She might have some bright ideas. Or be able to tell me the next useful chapter in my textbook. But then again, she is a bit dizzy. So maybe she won't. Funny. It's very quiet."

Wilma stopped and listened. The place was silent. Miss Lambard was nowhere to be heard or seen. She wasn't in the classrooms, she wasn't in the main hall, and her office, full of clutter, rope, and one old parachute, was empty of her too.

Wilma pondered, her lips pursing with thought.

Pickle, who could always be relied on in any manner of tricky situations, nudged his friend in the leg and pointed his nose upward toward a piece of paper pinned to the notice board. Wilma peered at it.

On an adventure until further notice. No homework till then. No milk till spring, please.

Thank you.

Wilma peered a bit harder. Her eyes widened. Her mouth dropped open. "Pickle," she whispered, pointing a shaking finger at the note. "Paper's homemade. Looks to be written with a thick nib. Bit messy. Smudges at the end of the sentences . . ."

Pickle gulped.

"This note," gasped Wilma, near incredulous, "was written by the same person who wrote the unfinished letter! Miss Lambard? Could it be? Is she my missing relative? Is she my aunt? Or is she just doing some undercover investigating for my missing relative? Either way, she's going to be able to provide the next piece in the puzzle, make no mistake! Oh my goodness! On an adventure till further notice! I can hardly bear it! Well," she added with a sudden and firm nod. "There's nothing I can do about her now. I shall have to wait. Mr. Goodman bided his time and so can I. And there's always the butcher's-muslin clue to follow up! I may be small, but I'm very determined."

Unpinning the precious clue from the notice

board, Wilma tucked it into her pinafore pocket. "This," she announced, holding a finger aloft, "is the next clue in the Case of the Missing Relative! And get to the bottom of it I shall! Nothing and nobody stops Wilma Tenderfoot!"

Pickle snorted. For nothing and nobody would stop him helping her do it.

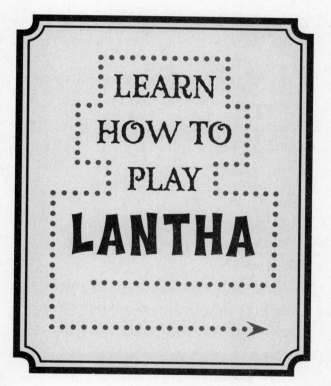

LEARN
HOW TO
PLAY
LANTHA

LANTHA INSTRUCTIONS

The Game:

Lantha: a game for two people. The object of the game is to get all your counters past the end Star square first to win. The loser must wear some (clean) underpants on their head for the rest of the day.

In order to get each counter home and off the board, you need to throw a number on the die that is at least one higher than you need to reach the Star square.

You will need: a six-sided die, five black counters, and five white counters.

Arrange the counters across the top of the Lantha board as indicated—whoever rolls highest begins. You must enter a new counter onto the board with each roll. Once all your counters are on the board, you can decide which ones to move with each throw of the die.

The Rules:

You can send an opponent's counter back to the start by landing on it, but only if it's a single counter. If two of the same counters are occupying the same square, they are both safe.

You cannot land on a square occupied by two or more of your opponent's counters.

THE HA-HA SEND A PIECE BACK SQUARE— You may send back to the start any one of your opponent's counters. If an opponent's counter is already on this square when you land on it, it automatically goes back to the start, plus one other counter of your choice.

THE DOUBLE UP SQUARE—Landing on this square means you can also bring one other counter, of your choosing, to the square (which makes them both safe). There is no limit to how many counters can be on this square at any one time. If you only have two counters left on the board and the second one is in front, then you must bring it back.

THE PICK YOUR NOSE SQUARE—If you land on this square you must pick your nose. Failure to pick noses will result in instant disqualification.

THE PICK SOMEONE ELSE'S NOSE SQUARE—Bad luck! You must pick your opponent's nose!

THE MISS A TURN SQUARE—You must miss a turn!

THE MOO SQUARE—You must make the noise of any farmyard animal. Loudly.

THE DANCE LIKE YOUR DAD SQUARE—Stand up and dance like a grown-up with no natural rhythm for at LEAST ten seconds.

THE SHAKE YOUR BUM SQUARE—Shake your bum for five seconds.

THE TICKLE SQUARE—Landing on this square means that your opponent must tickle you for a sustained period or until you beg for mercy.

THE GO FIVE FORWARD SQUARE—Move any counter five spaces forward.

THE GO FIVE BACK SQUARE*—Move any counter five spaces back.

THE GO BACK TO START SQUARE—The one counter that lands on this square must go all the way back to the beginning . . .

THE SEND ALL PIECES BACK SQUARE—ALL your single counters must go back to the start. Same counters in stacks of two or more are safe.

* When you get bored of moving forward and backward between the Five Forward and Five Back squares, you may move six spaces back.

LANTHA
START
MOOOO!
MISS A TUR
DANCE LIKE YOUR DAD
SHAKE YOUR BUM
HA-HA! Send back opponent's piece
GO BACK TO START
Pick somec else's n
SEND ALL PIECES BACK
TICKLE!
DOUBLE UP!

BOARD ☆

Turn the page for a chapter
of the next book in the series . . .

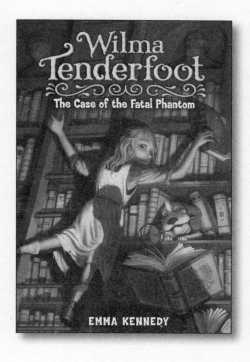

Something ominous was on the wind. Wilma looked up, wayward braids billowing, and pulled her scarf tighter. The sky had turned a menacing yellow and had rolled over Cooper Island's one small hill like a heavy pie crust so that everything felt hemmed in and swallowed up.

"Mrs. Speckle says there'll be snow, Pickle," said Wilma. "And lots of it." Pickle, Wilma's pet beagle and best friend, tried to look up, but Mrs. Speckle, the ever-stubborn and wool-obsessed housekeeper at Clarissa Cottage, had pulled an old tea cozy over his head to keep him warm, which was all very well but meant he couldn't see. He did his best to peer through the end of the narrow woolen spout, though. It was far from ideal.

"Now then," said Wilma, making her way to the bottom of the garden. "We've got to get parsnip heads and sprout tops for Brackle Day. And the only place we're going to find them is in the compost heap. And Pickle," she added, turning and shooting her dog a serious stare, "you have to help me *find* them. Not *eat* them." Pickle snorted. He loved compost. It was practically his favorite dinner. Maybe he could secretly snap up one parsnip head. Or maybe two. Or even *seven*.

The compost was contained in a series of large wooden crates at the rear of the garden. "Ooh pooh!" said Wilma, pinching her nose as they approached. "Compost stinks!" Pickle cocked his tatty ear, lifted his snout skyward, and sniffed the tangy stench. Yes, it did. Lovely! The crates were tall and raised off the ground on a platform of short stilts so that Wilma, who was small but determined for a ten-year-old, needed to work out how she could peer into them. She pursed her lips in thought and reached for the apprentice detective's notebook in her pinafore pocket.

Pickle scratched his ear. The tea cozy he was wearing was *really* itchy. "Hmm," said Wilma, looking at a glued-in picture of one of the old cases of her mentor, Detective Goodman. "In the Case of the Battered Cod, Mr. Goodman had to use a pulley system to move a heavy object over a vat of frying oil. That's it!"

Wilma tucked her notebook back into her pocket and looked around the garden. "There!" She pointed. "The clothesline! If we tie it in a loop, we can fix one end to the top of the fence post and attach the other end to the branch of the cherry tree. Then we can fix the ladder to the bottom line with garden twine, use two large spools to create the pulley, and it might just work!" She grinned down at Pickle. His tongue was sticking out of the end of the tea cozy.

After running back indoors to fetch two of

Mrs. Speckle's large spools, Wilma had her make-shift winching system rigged up in no time. The idea was that she would balance on the ladder while Pickle tugged the extra length of clothes-line. His pulling would cause the looped cord to rotate around the spools, which, in turn, would move Wilma and the ladder into position above the compost. From there, she could work out where the parsnip heads and sprout tops were, pick them out, and be winched back to safety. It was devilishly simple.

"Right, then, Pickle," said Wilma as she hopped onto the bottom rung of the ladder swinging from the lower part of the clothesline. "Take that slack piece of cord in your mouth and pull it till I tell you to stop."

Pickle, ears full of tea cozy, followed Wilma's pointing finger to the loose end of clothesline. Taking the cord in his mouth, he stared as she gabbled further instructions. He couldn't hear a word she was saying, of course, because of the wool, but from her gestures he thought he got the gist. So off he went. The cord he was carrying became taut and as Pickle took up the tension, the looped clothesline gave a little jerk. "That's it, Pickle!" shouted Wilma as she inched toward the compost. "Keep pulling!"

Pickle looked back over his shoulder and saw Wilma waving enthusiastically. She must want him to go a bit faster. Biting down on the cord, Pickle broke into a run, but the sudden wrench on the looped clothesline caused it to disconnect from the spools. Wilma, feeling the ladder lurch violently, looked up to see one of the makeshift pulleys ping upward into the air. "No, Pickle!" she yelled. "Stop! Oh no! STOP!" But Pickle couldn't hear her and instead ran a bit faster. The clothesline snapped away from the fence post, flinging Wilma and the ladder downward toward the compost. Clutching the ladder, she ricocheted against the front edge of the central compost crate but was then pitched backward so that she hit the container to her right. As she slowly slid downward into the heap of stinking and rotting matter, there was a deep groan from beneath her. The force of the impact had buckled the stilts below, and with a shuddering moan, the whole platform collapsed, sending the three compost crates and Wilma tumbling to the ground. Pickle stopped and turned around. Before him was a sea of compost, and sitting in the middle of it was Wilma.

"Well," she said, spitting out a mouthful of old potato peels, "this is some mess. Oh, wait. There's a parsnip head," she added, pulling one out from the front of her pinafore. "Pickle! Pass me the basket! Mr. Goodman says you sometimes have to get your hands dirty to get a job done. Well, I'm dirty all over, so that must mean the job will get done even quicker. Nothing and nobody stops Wilma Tenderfoot!" And with that, she flicked a piece of moldy bacon from her knee and began gathering up the vegetable bits she needed. Pickle looked on jealously. He'd *love* to be that filthy.

Wilma Tenderfoot, apprentice detective to Theodore P. Goodman, Cooper Island's most famous and serious detective, had plenty of enthusiasm and always did her best, but things never quite went according to plan. Despite all her efforts, she often seemed to find herself in a scrape or a muddle, especially ever since her hero, the mind-bogglingly brilliant detective Mr. Goodman, had taken her in, and accepted her as his apprentice. Abandoned at the gates of the Lowside Institute for Woeful Children when she was a baby, Wilma hadn't the least idea who she really was or where she had come from. For years she had dreamed of growing up to detect and deduct her own story, and there was no one she wanted to emulate more in doing so than the great Theodore P. Goodman. She'd been cutting out newspaper articles about him and studying all his cases since she was old enough to read. And now she lived with him at Clarissa Cottage and worked for him! It had been a month since their last case, a tricky assignment involving some putrid poison at a vaudeville the-atre and (another) near death-experience for Wilma, but Mr. Goodman had rescued her in the nick of time. Wilma was pleased that since then Cooper's Criminal Elements seemed to have been behaving themselves. But at the same time she found herself itching once more to advance her detecting skills and prove that she COULD get things right.

Cooper, an island somewhere between England and France and shaped like a bow tie, has never been discovered. There was once a close encounter with the great explorer Scott of the Antarctic, who almost landed there on his way to the North Pole, but as he had only packed winter clothes, he decided against it, reasoning that it looked "a bit warm." Since then, nobody from the outside world had ever come close to visiting and no one from Cooper had ever left. There were rumors that a slightly deranged man had once been found washed up on the rocks at Filthy Cove burbling in a language nobody could understand but Inspector Lemone, Theodore's right-hand man and Cooper's only policeman, always dismissed this as a "bag of nonsense" and said that it was "probably a large seal or hairy fish." And that was that.

Like all odd places, Cooper had its own traditions: There was the monthly Egg Nudge and the thrice-yearly Cow Stare, but the greatest day of all was Brackle Day, the once-a-year celebration of island life in which the great separation of the island into the Lowside (the woebegone part of the island) and the Farside (the well-to-do bit) was commemorated. Presents were hidden, Brackling Plays were performed across the island, and mighty feasts were enjoyed. As with all big days, preparations were required, and Wilma and Pickle had been tasked with the greatest responsibility of all—gathering up the decorations.

The Brackle Bush was a large, unwieldy, thickety thing with long poisonous thorns and stinging leaves. As plants go it was a menace, but because it had played an intrinsic part in the original separation of the island, every Cooperan was required to acquire one and put it in their parlor for the duration of Brackle Week. Tradition dictated that the Brackle Bush had to lean at a forty-five-degree angle, be covered in parsnip heads and sprout tops, and crowned with a magnificent giant corn-crumble biscuit, which, in fancy houses, was often decorated too. Sometimes the biscuits would be adorned with intricate marzipan paintings of Cooper landmarks like the one small hill or the broken plow at Wimpers Farm, but most people liked to decorate them with short motivational phrases like "Bend at the knees NOT the hips" or "If it's brown, flush it down." At Clarissa Cottage Mrs. Speckle, who was in charge of the icing, always decorated her corn crumble with the same two words—"Try harder"—because, as she said every year, "We can all do that. And I have a very small icing bag. Take it or leave it."

"You have some eggshell in your hair," said Mrs. Speckle, peering into the basket of vegetable tops Wilma and Pickle had brought back to Clarissa Cottage, "and a slug on your shoulder. But I can't be bothering with that now! I've got giant biscuits to make. And get Pickle into the Brackle Apron. That bush isn't going to decorate itself!"

Dogs, of course, are not normally called upon to perform decorating duties, but Cooper custom dictated that the Brackle Bush had to be prepared by the youngest member of the household, which in this case meant Pickle. He didn't have a clue about fancy arranging, draping, or dangling. Still, he'd have to do his best. The entire household was depending on him. And there was always a chance he could quietly sneak the odd sprout top when no one was looking.

Hounds have to put up with all manner of indignities. In his short time as Wilma's loyal dog, Pickle had been dressed as a plumber and forced to wear a tutu. Surely things couldn't get any worse? But as Wilma pulled the heavy Brackle Apron onto him, Pickle realized, with a sigh, that they could. The Brackle Apron was a bit like a large beach ball made of an impenetrable material that had to be blown up so that the Brackler, once inside it, was completely protected from the inevitable thorn pricks and leaf stings. As Wilma pumped with her foot, the apron inflated, and when she was finished, all that could be seen of the beagle was the end of his snout. "Good," she said with a nod. "Now you can get on with it. The basket of parsnip heads and sprout tops is there. Just pick them out with your mouth and put them on the bush. And I'd stop rolling onto your back if I were you. You'll never get anything done if you're upside down."

"Ah, Wilma," said a syrupy voice. It was Theodore P. Goodman, the most serious and famous detective that ever lived. He was tremendous to look at, with a mighty shock of golden hair, a chiseled jaw, and a mustache with caramel-colored tips—the very definition of swoony. "A parcel has arrived. Addressed to you." The great man stopped and sniffed the air, his magnificent mustache twitching in the firelight. "What's that *awful* smell?"

Wilma fidgeted and scraped at an unpleasant-looking stain on the front of her pinafore. "Probably the sprout tops," she said, thinking quickly.

"Hmm," replied Theodore. "It is a great shame we can't decorate our Brackle Bushes with things that are pleasantly fragrant. Still, tradition is tradition, however ridiculous it is." He stared at the inflated hound in front of him. "I see Pickle is this year's Brackler. Might get it done quicker if he can roll in the direction of the Brackle Bush. I think he's stuck under my bureau. You probably want to dislodge him, Wilma."

"Hang on. A parcel?" asked Wilma brightly, giving the bouncing Brackle Apron a small shove. "Is it a Brackle Day present? I'll have to give it to Mrs. Speckle to hide if it is."

Hiding presents seems a perfectly reasonable custom. In England presents are often hidden, sometimes beneath a bed or in a cupboard under some stairs. The hiding is merely a stopgap until such time as the present can be brought out and given to the person it's intended for. On Cooper, however, people *really* hide presents. They get buried, stuffed into cracks and crannies in perilous places, and sometimes even fed to sharks or crocodiles, because a person would have to be crazy to try to get back a soap-on-a-rope from a ten-foot reptile. And that's the point! On Cooper, the joy is in the hiding. And if the present is retrieved, well, the day has been ruined. Thankfully, Wilma's parcel was not a present. It came from her headmistress, Kite Lambard.

As an apprentice, Wilma had been enrolled at the Academy of Detection and Espionage, a venerable if slightly bizarre institution where she was the only pupil and her headmistress, Kite Lambard, the only teacher. The headmistress, however, had recently gone off on an adventure, leaving Wilma to her own devices. Many children might leap for joy at the prospect of going to a school with no teachers or lessons, but not Wilma. Not only did she want to learn the mysteries of detection, she also had some mysteries of her own, namely her family origins, to come to grips with, and without Kite's help she might as well be stuck in glue.

She had already unearthed some crucial evidence, and with a little guidance from her mentor, Theodore P. Goodman, had made a Clue Board for what she was calling the Case of the Missing

Relative. A Clue Board, Wilma had learned, was a vital tool for any detective: It was a quick visual summary of every piece of evidence gathered so far—a bit like a fridge door, but only covered in very serious things.

On her Clue Board Wilma had pinned the following:

1. The small tag that had been tied around her neck when she was left at the Institute, with the words "Because they gone" scrawled on it.

2. A scrap of muslin with a crest of crossed lamb chops on it that had been wrapped around her baby body. Penbert, the island's assistant forensic scientist, had also identified a stain on the material as being pig's blood.

3. One of the many notes given to Wilma by the revolting matron of the Institute for Woeful Children, Madam Skratch, listing monthly payments for Wilma's upkeep and referring to her as "Child 427." Now Wilma knew there was still someone alive who was either related to her or felt responsible for her, but WHO?

And why had they let her remain at the dreadful Institute for so long?

4. A page from an anonymous handwritten note to Madam Skratch asking about an abandoned baby, and

5. Wilma's most exciting clue—a note by Kite Lambard that appeared to be in the same handwriting as the anonymous note to Madam Skratch.

These were the beacons in the fog, the clues that would help Wilma piece together her past, discover who her parents were, and at last give her the sense of belonging that she had always longed for. However, until she saw her headmistress and asked her about that mysterious letter, she would be none the wiser. Wilma would have to be patient.

"There's a card stuck on the parcel, Mr. Goodman," said Wilma, blinking with excitement. "Look at the handwriting. It's definitely the same as that letter I found. Do you think Miss Lambard could be my missing relative?"

Theodore turned and reached for his pipe on

the mantelpiece. Slowly packing it with rosemary tobacco from the leather pouch in his waistcoat pocket, he frowned a little and pondered. "Remember, a good detective doesn't jump to conclusions, Wilma. Until you have spoken to Miss Lambard, there is no point in speculating."

"Does speckle-eating mean feeling fizzy in your tummy? Like when you've drunk too many Sugarcane Swizzles?" asked Wilma, twiddling the hem of her pinafore. "So that you can't concentrate and you think you might be a bit sick?"

"Not really," answered Theodore, sitting at his desk. "It means to guess or make your mind up about something when you don't have the full facts before you. Speculating is the very last thing an apprentice detective should do. It can cause a lot of bother."

"I see." Wilma nodded wisely, steering Pickle from behind the armchair. "Though it's quite hard not to." Having established that the parcel was not a Brackle Day present, Wilma ripped it open. "Oh," she said, eyes widening. "It's a study sheet. For detecting and spinach."

"Espionage," corrected Theodore, lighting his pipe.

"Yes, that." Wilma nodded again. "I expect Miss Lambard wanted to make sure I'm keeping up with my studies while she's away. And there's a piece of paper too," she added, unfolding it. " 'Dear Wilma, just to let you know I will be returning on Brackle Day for the traditional Academy Play. I am enclosing the cast list.' Oh, Mr. Goodman! Miss Lambard's coming back! I'll be able to ask her about that letter. But why has she sent me a cast list?"

"It's an Academy tradition, Wilma," replied Theodore, puffing out a plume of rosemary smoke. "Every pupil has to perform the Brackling Play. Consider it a rite of pass—"

"Ooooh!" Wilma interrupted. "I've been cast as Melingerra Maffling! I always wanted to be her when I was at the Institute! And I'm Old Jackquis. And Stavier Cranktop. And the Porpoise. Actually, I'm everyone. Except the Brackle Bush. That's you, Pickle! What do you think about that?"

But Pickle couldn't respond. He was rolling slowly but surely toward an old clue from Mr. Goodman's Case of the Krazy Knockout. It was an oversized boxing glove attached to the end of a very temperamental spring. Suddenly realizing what was about to happen, Theodore stood up. "Not there, Pickle! Quick, Wilma, grab him!" Wilma leaped forward but slid on a banana peel that had fallen from her shoulder and collided with Pickle, sending the inflated Brackle Apron careering even faster into the sprung boxing glove. With a deep *thwack* the glove exploded outward, punching Pickle across the room as fast as lightning.

"Oh no!" yelled Wilma as Pickle smashed into the untethered Brackle Bush, which, shuddering from the impact, quietly keeled over and fell into the open fireplace, where it burned to a crisp in an instant.

"Goodness," said Theodore, surveying the charred mess. "Well. We shall need a new Brackle Bush, Wilma, or there will be no celebrations for us."

Wilma stared at the small scene of devastation that she had had a part in causing yet again. One day, she thought to herself as she let the air out of an indignant Pickle's Brackle Apron, she would get something entirely right. She really would.